# June 1st 1939

This is the first ever diary of Her Royal Highness, Princess Margaret Rose.

Sometimes I wake early and can't get back to sleep, because my head's too full of things I want to do. So I thought it would be nice to have something to do that doesn't make a noise. I'm always getting told off for too much noise.

I have this chunky notebook with a photo of me and my sister, Lilibet, on the front. There are no dates in it, so it's not a proper diary, but that's good. It means I don't have to write in it every day. I get a bit fed up with things I have to do. There are far too many of those.

Ruby and Bobo, our nursery maids, and Alla, our nanny, are fast asleep. So is my sister.

Lilibet is Her Royal Highness, Princess Elizabeth, and she is a Very Important Person, because one day she'll be the Queen of England. Poor her, that's what I say.

She'll be a very good queen, because she's a very good person. She's sensible and obedient, and everyone considers her responsible and serious.

She's not a bit like me!

## June 21st

Oh dear, I'm not very organized about this diary business. It's weeks since I started it. But while Mummy and Papa have been away in Canada and America, our governess, Crawfie, has kept us so busy. Lilibet thinks Crawfie does it so we won't miss Mummy and Papa too much, but they've been gone more than six weeks. That's a long time to be without your mother and father. But when your parents are the King and Queen of England, you must expect sad times and just keep smiling. It isn't always easy.

We have lessons, of course, and walks, but we've also had lots of outings to keep us cheerful. The best ones were a boat trip on the River Thames, visits to the Royal Tournament and the Royal Mint (we were presented with some special coins), and some glorious picnics.

The most exciting outing was a ride on an underground train! Lilibet and I call it the tube, because that's what the people who use it every day call it. I tried to pretend I was a working lady, but it was difficult because there were policemen with us, and photographers kept calling out. Crawfie was very proper and just walked us straight through the crowd. I was allowed to hold my own ticket.

But there's another exciting outing planned for early tomorrow! Mummy and Papa are sailing home and we are to sail to meet them!

I can't wait.

## June 22nd

I'm supposed to be resting for ten minutes while Mummy and Papa say goodbye to the captain of this ship. It's called *Empress of Britain*, which is sort of what Mummy is!

This morning Lilibet and I sailed on a Royal Navy destroyer called HMS *Kempenfelt*. It was so exciting when at last we saw Mummy and Papa waving to us. We were so happy to see them again – so happy I almost forgot to curtsey! I'm glad I remembered, because lots of people were watching. Mummy always says it's important for us to behave properly in public. Lilibet never makes a mistake, but then, she always behaves properly, even in private.

When we were alone, we had such hugs! Papa said I've grown, which I'm pleased about. It's not nice being the smallest person in the palace.

Everyone talked at once, and then it was lunchtime. The ship's saloon was decorated with dozens of balloons. It was so bright and happy. And that was just how I felt inside – full of balloons!

The captain took us on to the bridge as we sailed towards the harbour. The bridge is where they drive the ship. It looked very complicated, but I didn't have a chance to examine all the dials and buttons. Papa drew Lilibet and me forward so we could join them in waving to all the people who had come to welcome him and Mummy home.

It looks as if every person in Britain has come to Southampton!

Next we're travelling to London by train.

## June 23rd

Crawfie came and spoke to Alla this morning. I was so tired I could hardly open my eyes.

Then Alla whispered, 'No lessons this morning, Margaret.' She's allowed to call me 'Margaret' in private. 'Her Majesty told Miss Crawford you need to rest.'

I suddenly remembered yesterday. I leapt out of bed and ran to shake Lilibet. 'Wake up! Let's go and see Mummy and Papa!'

She sat up. 'May we, Alla?'

Alla nodded. 'His Majesty sent a message to say he can't wait to see his girls!'

What fun we had! It was just like in the old days in our house in Piccadilly, before Papa became King and we moved to Buckingham Palace. Lilibet's too grown up for pillow fights (she's thirteen), but I'm not!

It's so lovely to have us four all together. Papa couldn't stop grinning as we rode home in the carriage from the station yesterday. I was silly to think that every person in Britain was in Southampton. There were thousands more on the London pavements. Mummy said her arm ached from waving. I don't know how she manages to keep smiling without stopping. I can't. It makes my face ache. Also, Lilibet and I rode facing backwards, which always makes me feel peculiar, what with the carriage bouncing and the horses' heads bobbing as the guardsmen ride alongside. Then it was upstairs for a balcony appearance.

Before we stepped on to the balcony, Lilibet said, 'Remember not to push to the front, Margaret. The people have come to see Mummy and Papa, not us.'

She shoved me in the right direction. Helpful, but irritating. I got my own back by being last to leave the balcony, and turning to give the people a final wave. Lilibet kept smiling, but I think she was annoyed.

## June 27th

Lilibet knows about my diary. She came up behind me while I was lying on the floor, writing. She didn't say anything, and she's never mentioned it. See? She's such a good person. I'd have asked about it if it had been hers, and I know my fingers would have been itching to get hold of it. But not Lilibet. She tries so hard to behave well, and she'd think it was sneaky to take a peek.

But still, I'll keep it hidden. These are my true thoughts, and I'm sure there'll be some I'd rather people didn't see.

I must change now for swimming. We're entering some races at the Swimming Bath Club in Mayfair on Thursday. It's fun there, because we swim with other children. We're usually allowed time to just mess around, as Ruby calls it, and it's so much better when there's more than two of us. Lilibet says I shouldn't grumble about us being alone, because we're fortunate to have our own swimming pool here in the palace. Most children only go to the public baths – if they're lucky. I didn't think about that until she said it.

# Later

We did really well, considering we're not used to racing. Mummy presented the prizes, of course, and there were lots of photographs. All those flashing lights! I got a silver cup and Lilibet got a shield. We were going to put them on the nursery mantelpiece, but Papa said they must have pride of place in the drawing room. He's such a darling.

Wouldn't it be lovely if every country had a king like Papa? I feel sorry for the German people. They don't have a king or queen. Instead they have a leader called Herr Adolf Hitler. Although Mummy and Papa don't discuss him much, one of the footmen, who we really like, said, 'I expect His Majesty will talk about nothing else but Herr Hitler when he meets the prime minister today.' He was taking the dogs for a run and Lilibet and I tagged along. Not everybody likes our corgis, because they can be snappy, but he does. He takes a ball and plays with them. That's why we like him. I call him Buttons, because he looks just like Buttons in my *Cinderella* book.

Lilibet said, 'Herr Hitler's a bad man, isn't he?' and Buttons said, 'He's bad for Germany, that's for sure, Ma'am, and he's bad news for us, he is. That's if there's a war.'

War. Ugh. Horrid word.

After tea, Lilibet and I went upstairs to groom our horses. We keep them on the nursery landing. Some are on wheels, and some stand on their own four legs. They all have saddles and bridles. We groom them all every evening, and feed them and give them water. Well, not really, of course, just pretend. We know how to do it properly, because we watch the grooms look after our ponies when we've been riding.

Actually, Lilibet sometimes sits on the floor with her back against the wall and cuddles Dookie or Jane or one of the other dogs. She doesn't play much these days. It's because she's almost grown up. She even wears silk stockings, instead of socks. I'm glad I don't, because I'd rip them to shreds in no time. But what fun to be grown up. Parties, music and dancing, and lovely clothes, too. And visits to the ballet!

## July 15th

We're off to sea again! Papa says the royal yacht is almost as old as he is, and this is probably our last chance to sail in her. We're going to visit the Royal Naval College at Dartmouth, in Devon, where Papa did part of his naval training.

# July 22nd

We've had a lovely trip so far, except that Lilibet and I are expected to carry on with lessons while we're travelling. Honestly, we never get a holiday from work. Lilibet groaned when she realised it was arithmetic first (she didn't let Crawfie hear), so I decided to waste time. 'Crawfie,' I said, 'I simply must tell you about my dream last night!'

The dream was actually quite dull, and I can hardly remember it. But I did what Crawfie always tells me to do, and used my imagination. She kept saying, 'Oh, Margaret, do stop,' and, 'Margaret, don't be ridiculous,' but I know she enjoyed my tale. Lilibet struggled not to laugh, because she knew what I was up to. It worked. We wasted nearly half the lesson!

Later on some of the officers taught us a dance called the Lambeth Walk. The best bit was that every time the words went '… doing the Lambeth Walk', we all had to shout 'Oy!' They said I picked up the steps really quickly. I think Lilibet did, too. When they taught us another dance, the Palais Glide, we joined together and danced in a row. It was more difficult than the Lambeth Walk. Lilibet did better than me because she concentrates more than I do, but we both ended up laughing at the way our legs kept getting muddled.

The ship sailed into the River Dart, and we moored near Dartmouth Castle. Our ship, the *Victoria and Albert*, is surrounded all the time by dozens of sailing and rowing boats. They look like toys compared to our ship. They're full of friendly people, waving and cheering. Dartmouth is a pretty village, with painted cottages clinging to the hillside. I wanted to leap ashore and run up the hill, but we had to be received officially at the castle's quay. Lots of hands to shake. As usual, I was the last in the shaking-hands line. Papa's first, being the King, then Mummy, then Lilibet – partly because she's older than me, but especially because she's the heir to the throne. As I said, she's a Very Important Person. I'm just number two in line for the throne.

Tomorrow we visit the college. Papa's second cousin, Uncle Dickie – he's really Lord Louis Mountbatten – is dining on board tonight.

## July 23rd

What a lovely day! It's been so much fun. Lilibet says it's been one of the nicest days she's ever had in her life. (And I know why!!!)

As it's Sunday, we were supposed to attend a service in the college chapel, but Uncle Dickie sent a message saying that Lilibet and I shouldn't go, because some of the cadets have mumps. I once saw someone with mumps, and it wasn't a pretty sight. He had great swellings each side of his face, and Mummy said the poor boy felt really ill. I don't want that. What's worse is you have to stay indoors for absolutely ages, resting, which would be ghastly.

So off Mummy and Papa went, escorted by some very smart cadets. They're young men who are training to become naval officers.

Lilibet and I were taken to the Captain's House to wait for our parents. The captain's the person in charge of the college. His family are the Dalrymple-Hamiltons, who we haven't met before.

We both felt shy, being in a strange place, but we were introduced to a tall, fair-haired cadet, called Prince Philip of Greece and Denmark. Uncle Dickie had sent him to the Captain's House to amuse us. He's a second or third cousin of ours – I can never work them out, but Queen Victoria is his ancestor, which is the same as us. She's our great-great-grandmother.

To be honest, I think Philip's a bit of a show-off. But it doesn't matter, because he's good fun. He got the Dalrymple-Hamiltons' train set going, and both Lilibet and I had lots of goes. Afterwards, we went for a walk, and when we reached the tennis court, Philip said, 'Let's jump the net!'

I would have had a go, but it was too high and, anyway, we weren't wearing the sort of clothes you can jump nets in. Lilibet wouldn't have jumped it, whatever she was wearing, not at any price. She doesn't do that sort of thing. But Philip did! Over and over he jumped (showing off).

He's a bit of a tease, and he kept picking on me. I didn't mind. He makes me laugh.

We played croquet, too. It was so draughty up on the hill that we had to keep our coats on. Lilibet's a good player – it's quite hard to be bad at croquet – and she thought Philip was good, too. She kept watching him. In my opinion he cheated, and I told her so.

'He isn't cheating,' she hissed. 'Don't be so rude, Margaret.'

I watched his mallet and his feet, not his face, and I say he cheated. Still, everyone cheats at croquet, don't they? It's part of the fun.

Philip was invited to lunch, and he was friendly with everyone. Mummy said, 'You've met Elizabeth before, Philip, at the wedding of her uncle George, the Duke of Kent. Do you remember?'

'Of course I do, Ma'am,' he said, but he changed the subject quickly, so I don't think that was true. After all, she was only four. Why would he remember her?

Later that evening, I said to Lilibet, 'Wouldn't it be lovely if Philip lived in London? We could become friends.'

She went pink and said, 'Yes, that would be nice.'

I looked her right in the eye until she couldn't help laughing. She really likes Philip, I can tell.

## July 24th

Prince Philip joined us for dinner on the *Victoria and Albert* last night. Either they don't feed the cadets very well, or that boy has the most enormous appetite! He ate and ate and finally polished off a huge banana split. He even finished before me!

Lilibet and I talked in bed last night.

'He's a very good-looking boy, isn't he?' she said.

In fact, she talked about him quite a bit. It's odd, because he's not the sort of person she normally likes. He's bouncy and, well, boisterous, Crawfie says. Lilibet usually likes calm, quiet people. Except for me. I'm not usually calm or quiet, and she loves me.

# July 25th

We left Dartmouth to a very rowdy send-off. The cadets came out in little boats to escort us downriver to the sea. There were so many buzzing round our ship, Papa was worried that someone might get hurt, and asked for them to be sent back to shore.

All the little boats, with the cadets still waving, turned towards shore. All except one. It was easy to guess who that was. Prince Philip of Greece and Denmark!

Papa was cross. 'Young idiot!' he said. Mummy just smiled, and Lilibet and I waved like mad.

An officer shouted at Philip over the loudspeaker, and he finally turned his boat away from us. But he never stopped waving.

When we went below (that means downstairs), Crawfie said he was too full of himself. Lilibet said, 'He is rather, Crawfie,' but I said, 'Well, I think he's fun.' And when Crawfie left, I whispered to Lilibet, 'You do, too, don't you?'

She went pink again.

# July 31st

I feel scared, but a little excited, too, because we might have a war against Germany. There was one about twenty years ago, and it lasted four years. Our soldiers fought in places like France and Belgium, and it was utterly ghastly, Crawfie says.

Mummy and Papa don't talk to us about war. They don't like to worry us. At least, they don't talk to me, but I do think they talk to Lilibet. I expect she needs to know about these things, for when she becomes queen.

I'm glad I won't be queen. I don't like thinking about nasty things. And I'd hate to have to be serious all the time, like Papa. Well, most of the time. He's always lots of fun when he's with me. I like to make him laugh.

# August 1st

We'll be late going to Scotland for the summer, and it's all that awful Mr Hitler's fault. This war business is spoiling everything. When I said that to Lilibet, she said, 'Oh, Margaret, you don't understand. Papa's meetings with the prime minister are far more important than a little girl's summer holiday.'

It annoys me when she says I don't understand. And it really annoys me that she says it so nicely that I can't get cross with her.

I just hope we get to Balmoral in time for my birthday. We actually stay at Birkhall, which is cosier than Balmoral Castle, but very close to it. It's not quite as tartan as the castle, which even has tartan carpets and curtains. Too much tartan makes my eyes go fuzzy.

## August 22nd

It's all horrible. Papa came to lunch looking very serious.

'My loves,' he said, 'I'm afraid I have to leave Scotland. I must return to London tonight.'

'Why?' I asked. 'Is it Mr Hitler again?'

'In a way,' he said. 'Germany and Russia have joined together, and that's not a good thing.'

Poor Papa. Poor Mummy, too. She never grumbles. She keeps on smiling. I shall try to keep smiling, too.

## August 25th

We all went for a lovely ride this morning. It was misty, and I love riding in the mist. I imagine I'm one of King Arthur's knights. Mummy was late, as usual, and I thought the sun might break through before we got going, but it didn't.

Before we turned for home, Lilibet called, 'Margaret, see that tree with a drooping branch?'

'Yes.'

'Race you!' And she was off. That was annoying because it gave her a good start.

'Cheat!' I yelled, as I kicked my pony on. We thundered along, catching up with Lilibet quite easily.

While she was still just ahead, she made the mistake of slowing down as she reached the tree. But I kept up speed and passed Lilibet right at the last moment, simply by charging past the tree and cantering round in a wide circle, back to where she was.

'I won!' I said. It felt good to be better than Lilibet at something.

Mummy laughed and told me I rode too hard, because my face was as red and shiny as a ripe tomato!

Lilibet doesn't mind losing, as long as the person who wins plays fairly. She gets cross with herself, though, if she doesn't do as well as she knows she can.

## August 26th

Mummy had some news at tea time and I didn't like it.

'I had a long talk with Papa on the telephone last night,' she said, 'and I feel that he needs me with him in London.'

'Oh no!' I said.

'Hush, Margaret,' said Lilibet. 'Mummy must have a good reason.'

'But we've only been here for about two weeks,' I said. 'It's not fair that we have to go.' I made the sad face I use when I want Mummy to know I'm really, really upset. It sometimes helps me to get my way.

Mummy smiled. 'You're not going. I shall go, and I'll be back before you know it. You'll have a lovely time with Crawfie and Alla fussing over you. Picnics, rides, friends to stay … all manner of good things.'

'Goody!' I said, and then I felt bad, because I thought I'd hurt Mummy's feelings. She knows I don't want her to go, but I'm glad Lilibet and I are staying. Some cousins are coming to stay soon, but not for a while, so thank goodness for sisters!

## August 29th

I was miserable last night. I have a sore gum, and it hurts to eat. Alla says it's a little mouth ulcer and it will soon go. Little! It feels huge when I run my tongue over it. I'm sure I can feel a dent in the top, like a volcano.

Lilibet was kind to me. 'I wish I had the ulcer instead of you,' she said.

'I wish you did, too,' I said, but then I felt mean.

It was such a beautiful, sunny day today. Our cousin Margaret Elphinstone has arrived. She's a lot older than me. I think she's about fourteen, so she's nearer Lilibet's age. But it doesn't matter, because she plays just as much with me. She's fun.

Crawfie drove us in the pony-cart to the village, and bought us some sweets. I love sweets. I usually finish them quickly. Lilibet doesn't. Today I sucked instead of crunching, because of my little mouth ulcer. My sweets lasted much longer than usual! Some village children watched as we left the shop. I waved, and they gave tiny waves back. I suppose they can go to the village shop whenever they like, lucky things.

## September 3rd

A really bad thing is happening. Our country is at war with Germany. Or should that be against Germany? Mummy and Papa are really upset. The news came over the wireless. Germany has invaded Poland, and bombed their biggest city, Warsaw.

Lilibet took me for a walk down to the stables, and told me not to worry. 'Will they bomb London?' I asked.

She put her arm round me. 'You mustn't be frightened, Margaret,' she said. 'We have a fine army protecting us. And our Royal Navy and Air Force.' She smiled. 'We'll be well looked after.'

I thought about the guardsmen on duty outside our palace. They wouldn't be much help against bombs.

'Papa's going to be very busy,' said Lilibet, 'so we must be good.'

After tea, cousin Margaret, Lilibet and I tried to imagine what the war will be like. I sort of pictured swords and armour, like King Arthur, but the others said I was silly.

'In the Great War,' Lilibet said, 'thousands of young men died in trenches.'

'I've seen pictures,' said cousin Margaret. 'It was horrendous. Thick mud and shooting and explosions. The men lived in damp clothes and they hardly ever had a bath. I heard their feet rotted because they were wet all the time.'

I hope it's a very quick war. I hope none of our brave soldiers is killed.

## September 4th

Papa made a speech on the wireless last night. He spoke well, though slowly. My poor papa does find it so hard to speak sometimes, and he has help for his important speeches from a man called Mr Logue. Papa has trouble getting certain words out. Not when he reads us stories, though! He reads almost perfectly, then, and he's wizard at doing the voices.

After they played the national anthem, Lilibet asked, 'Do you think people stand for the national anthem when they hear it on the wireless, as they do in theatres?'

I got the giggles. 'Imagine people all over the country having dinner, and suddenly leaping to their feet! There'd be napkins and runner beans all over the floor!'

That earned me a stern look from Mummy. When I got a chance, I whispered to her that it was Lilibet who made me giggle.

My sister saw me. 'What's she saying, Mummy?'

Mummy waved a hand. 'Nothing, darling. Just Margaret being Margaret.'

Crawfie told us thousands of children are being evacuated. They're leaving London to live in the country. I'm sure they'll love the countryside, especially the children who live in tiny houses in crowded streets. But I'm sad for them, because they'll miss their parents. I know how bad that is, because Lilibet and I miss Mummy and Papa when they go away.

When I said I understood how the children felt, Lilibet said, 'You think you understand, Margaret, but it's so different for us. When Mummy and Papa go away, we still have Crawfie and Alla and a whole army of people looking after us. And we speak to Mummy and Papa every day, even when they're abroad. Those children have gone to live with strangers, and many of them don't have a telephone. Imagine that!'

I can't imagine that. I do hope the children have a sister or brother, at least.

## September 5th

We have blackout now. That means all the windows have thick black curtains over them, so no light shows through. Mummy said on the telephone that we must never open our curtains at night to peep out, if the lights are on. The reason for the blackout is so German pilots can't see where the cities are.

I told Lilibet I thought it was a waste of time. 'If I was a German pilot,' I said, 'I'd fly over during the day, when I could see everything.'

She laughed. 'Then you'd be shot down,' she said.

I don't like the sound of this war business. I hate Mummy and Papa being away. I'm glad I have my sister. She's sensible, and she always makes me feel better. Well, she tries to.

I thought cousin Margaret might want to go home, but she's happy to stay. We're going to play circuses tomorrow out in the field. Lilibet will be the ringmaster. She always is. I expect I'll be the dear little naughty pony. Cousin Margaret says that suits me perfectly. What colossal cheek (as Papa would say)!

# September 6th

Lilibet has been thinking about Prince Philip! I know she has, because she asked Papa on the phone today what would happen to all those fine cadets at Dartmouth, now we're at war. She told me what he said.

'All those who are trained will join the Royal Navy and be posted to ships.'

'Will they fight?' I asked.

'Of course,' said Lilibet. 'We must all defend our country.'

I don't know how much defending two young princesses can do.

'Our cousin Philip will go to sea,' she said. 'I shall write to him.'

Lilibet is very, very good about writing letters. I'm not so good. I mean to write, but there's usually something more interesting to do, and I have to be nagged. Then when I do make an effort, I get told off for not writing more than I absolutely have to. That's not fair. If I'm writing a thank-you letter, surely the most important bit is the thank-you. I can't imagine our grandmother, Queen Mary, wanting to read a lot of chit-chat about what I had for tea. Mummy says that's not the point, and Lilibet agrees. That's hardly surprising, as Granny thinks I'm spoilt, but she's always sweet to Lilibet, who is her pet.

I get annoyed when Lilibet sides with other people. Sisters should stick together.

## Later

I was thinking about sisters sticking together. I used to think that Lilibet and I would always be together. But there will be a time when we can't. One day, when we're quite grown up, Lilibet will have to be queen. Her life will change, and she'll rule the country and the Commonwealth, and be Empress of India. What will I be? I'll just be Princess Margaret Rose. I'll stay the same, for always. Unless I marry a king, of course. But I'm not doing that. It would mean living in another land, away from Mummy and Papa and Lilibet. Oh no.

But if I'm going to stay a princess, I shall make sure I can do all the things I want to when I grow up. I'll go to theatres, and ballets, and balls and parties. I don't want somebody else deciding what I do.

Poor Lilibet won't be able to say, 'I think I'll go to the ballet this evening.' All her outings will have to be planned, like Mummy's and Papa's are.

When I'm grown up, I'll have my own apartment in the palace, so I can see Mummy and Papa every day, but if I want to go out I'll just order the car and go. I won't ask anybody.

When my sister is queen, I shall show her this diary – well, bits of it – and she'll remember what it was like when we could play and have fun together.

## October 1st

I was grumbling today because I had to wear a pink skirt and jacket which I don't like, and Crawfie said I was selfish, and I should think of the poor evacuees. Some of them don't even have pyjamas or a change of clothes, and the kind country people who look after them have to find things for them from somewhere. I would willingly let them have the pink skirt and jacket.

Lilibet had a letter from a London friend who's gone to live at her family's country house for the war. They have evacuees staying in cottages in their park.

'What are the evacuees like?' I asked.

'Quite good fun, actually,' said Lilibet. 'But Susan says they've hardly ever seen proper fresh food before. She says they appear to live on fish and chips at home.'

There are fish-and-chip shops in London. I've seen people eating out of newspaper as we've driven past. It smells delicious!

## October 13th

I can't believe how long it is since I wrote in my diary. I've forgotten half of what we've been doing. Mummy and Papa come up to Birkhall to see us as often as possible. I told Crawfie and Lilibet that when they arrive tomorrow I'm going to beg them not to go back to London.

Crawfie took me to one side and said, 'Their Majesties would much rather be here with you, dear, but they have their duty to do. The King must be close to his government, and he needs the Queen with him.'

'I need them with me,' I said.

'Of course you do, but you have people around you who love you. Spare a thought for the evacuees, who have no family with them.'

I do feel sorry for those children. I wish they could all come and live at Birkhall and be looked after like me.

Later on, Lilibet and I went into the kitchen garden to look for the last raspberries, and she made me promise not to whinge to Mummy and Papa about them coming back. 'Everybody's doing their bit for the war effort, Margaret,' she said. 'We can do our bit by being good and not worrying them. They have a lot to worry about already, you know.'

Right then, I decided. I'll do my bit, too. I won't make Mummy and Papa feel bad about leaving us here. I'll do my best to be cheerful and make them happy. I'm good at making people laugh.

## October 14th

Lilibet practically made our eyes stand out on stalks today. We were all together in the drawing room, and the wireless was on. The announcer said that one of our battleships, the *Royal Oak*, had been torpedoed by a German U-boat – that's a submarine.

Lilibet leapt out of her chair. I've never seen her so angry. Her fists were clenched, and she went on about 'all those sailors' and how wicked the U-boat captain was. It's really unusual for her to get het up like that.

I said, 'Come and sit beside me, Lilibet,' and I held her hand. She sat with her lips pressed together, and then picked up her knitting. Mummy's taught us not to show our emotions in public. Even if we're upset, we mustn't cry or get cross. I thought perhaps Lilibet was annoyed with herself for being angry, even though we were in private.

I told her a joke about an elephant and three oranges, but she didn't laugh. So much for trying to cheer people up. It doesn't always work.

### Later

I said I wished the evacuees could come and live at Birkhall, and they are! Well, not in our house, obviously. They're living in cottages on the Balmoral estate, though. We'll meet them one day.

### November 10th

Mummy said we mustn't complain if we don't always get the food we like. All sorts of things will be rationed, she said, like sugar and butter and bacon.

Lilibet said, 'But we get lots of our food from our own

farms and gardens, so we'll be all right,' and Mummy said, 'Yes, darling, we shall. Remind me, where is our sugar plantation?' Lilibet couldn't help laughing, but I was wondering about things like icing on birthday cakes, and sugar mice at Christmas.

## November 11th

Mummy made a speech on the wireless today to the women of the British Empire. The whole household listened, and everyone nodded and smiled and said her voice sounded beautiful. It always does. Lilibet says she has the sweetest voice in the world, especially when she laughs, and I agree.

## November 19th

There's a show in London at the Victoria Palace Theatre. I wish we could go. It's called *Me and My Gal*, and they do the Lambeth Walk in it.

'We're experts at that,' said Lilibet, and we taught it to

cousin Margaret. She's tall and thin, and as elegant as a grown-up dancer.

We must have looked funny, as we're all different shapes and sizes. Alla laughed at us, so we made her join in, then Crawfie came and she did, too.

I bet we're as good as the dancers on the stage. I bet I could be in that show. Wouldn't that be wonderful! I absolutely love to sing. I'd need some singing lessons, though, I expect.

## November 28th

Our cousin Margaret's going home in a few days. She says she'll miss us, and we'll miss her, too. We rode out today, and the ponies were especially frisky. It must have been the sunshine, as the weather's been gloomy lately. Afterwards, Lilibet stayed in the yard when Margaret and I went to get hot drinks. As long as she's wrapped up, she doesn't care about the weather. She adores being with horses.

One of the footmen told Ruby he went past a pub yesterday and the people were all singing 'Rule, Britannia'. Everyone's proud to be British, she says.

Lilibet just peeped out of the window. 'There's going to be a frost,' she said. 'It'll be chilly tomorrow.' Of course it will.

It's November. It's Scotland. Oh, how I long for London and our own garden. It never seems quite so cold there.

## December 2nd

Lilibet's allowed to stay up tonight to listen to the last *Bandwagon* programme. I'm not. I'm cross. I refuse to go to sleep until she comes up. I know she has to do some special things because of learning to be queen, but listening to the wireless isn't one of them.

## December 4th

Papa has gone to visit the troops in France. I won't breathe until he's back. Lilibet's worried, too. She listens to the news whenever she's allowed to.

## December 7th

Scotland is the coldest place in winter. The ground was so white this morning I truly thought it had snowed in the night. But it was simply frost. Not the thin frost we get in London – it's really thick. Our windows are covered in it by morning, and today my bath sponge was frozen. Ruby said she could crack walnuts with it.

When Papa comes home, I'll choose the right moment to ask if I can have proper singing lessons.

## December 10th

Papa's safely home. He actually went to the Front, where the fighting is. I think they have a line of British soldiers, with German ones opposite, and that's the Front. Papa went into a trench and he met the president and got a French medal.

## December 16th

Hurrah! The day after tomorrow we're off to Sandringham for Christmas with Mummy and Papa! I hope Norfolk's not as cold as Scotland.

In the morning, Crawfie's taking us to Woolworths to buy Christmas presents. Shopping's so exciting. Most children can do it any day of their lives if they want to, but we hardly ever do. Perhaps they get bored with shopping. I never would!

Lilibet said, 'You must make a list, Margaret, of the people you want to buy presents for. You could also note down any ideas you have.'

Lists are boring. What I'd really like is to have Crawfie take us into Woolworths and say to the manager, 'Their Royal Highnesses may wander among the counters by themselves for hours, and buy whatever they wish.' But that won't happen. Mummy says princesses have many privileges (I used to think that meant toys) so they shouldn't complain if there's something they can't have, or can't do.

I often wonder what life is like for children who aren't

royal. Do they ever wonder about us? Lilibet thinks they do. She says we must always set them a good example. That can be quite trying.

## December 27th

I'm worn out. We've had so many guests, and we've sung and danced and played games till we're all exhausted! Christmas is when Lilibet and I make all the grown-ups join in when we play charades or cards or sardines. It gets quite noisy!

I wish we could keep the Christmas tree for ever.

Christmas Day meant Papa speaking on the wireless. He wore his admiral's uniform for the photographs, and looked very handsome. There were a couple of sticky stammering bits which made us hold our breath, but then he got going and it was lovely, thanks to all his hard work and Mr Logue's. I am so proud of Papa.

Mummy gave Lilibet and me a gift of a beautiful leather diary, and she asked us to write in it every day. I'm not good at remembering to do things, and I'm sure I shan't always be able to think of things to write. It will probably end up something like: 'Ate breakfast. Did geography. Drank orange juice. Played outside. Had drawing lesson. Went for a walk.

Had tea with Mummy and Papa. Groomed ponies. Read a story. Went to bed.'

Lilibet says she'll remind me to write in my diary. I'm sure she will. She doesn't forget things like that, and if Mummy asks her to do something, she does it. She's very obedient. I'm sure that sometimes she thinks, 'Oh, botheration!' when she's told to do something, but she'd never say it. I would.

I'll still keep my secret diary. I can always say, 'Botheration!' in here!

## December 31st

Lilibet told me she's had several letters from Prince Philip. I never knew! He's in the Royal Navy now, so is quite grown up.

I'm going to write to him, too. I told Lilibet and she said I'm too young to be writing to boys. I said, 'He's not a boy, he's a cousin,' and that made her laugh.

It's the end of the year – the year the war began. I hope next year will be the year it ends.

Today I asked Papa about singing lessons. He said not just at the moment.

I was upset, but Lilibet said, 'Come on, Margaret. Put on a brave face.'

I made such a silly face that she spluttered with laughter, and everyone turned to look at her. That made her go red.

'Stop it at once,' she said.

'You must get used to being stared at if you're going to be queen!' I said.

Now Papa made a face. 'I hope that won't be for a long time yet!'

I felt sick. I'm always teasing Lilibet about when she's queen. I never thought. For her to become Queen Elizabeth, my darling papa would have to be

I can't write it. It makes tears come, just thinking about it.

## January 15th 1940

It's soooo cold. That's the bad news. The good news is that we're soon going to move to Royal Lodge, at Windsor. It's our country home, and we've always spent weekends there. Our ponies are there, and there's lots of space for the dogs, so it will be lovely. We're going to live there until the war's over. Although it's in Windsor Great Park, it's about three miles from Windsor Castle, which is in the Home Park.

Papa still has to be in London some of the time, and go out on visits, so Mummy will be going with him, but they've promised to come to Royal Lodge for the night whenever they can. That will be lovely. Much better than being so far away in Scotland.

## January 19th

Lilibet and I have our own ration books. Mine says 'Name: Her Royal Highness Princess Margaret Rose', and for my address, it says 'The Royal Lodge, Windsor Great Park.'

## February 7th

Royal Lodge isn't pink any more! The house has been painted a gloomy nothing sort of colour. That's to camouflage it. A German bomber could easily spot a pink house in a park. Mummy absolutely hates the colour, but she says she'll think of England and grin and bear it.

The first thing Lilibet and I did was run down to see Y Bwthyn Bach, which is Welsh for 'The Little House'. The people of Wales gave it to us. I was only two when it arrived, so I don't remember seeing it for the first time. Lilibet remembers, though. It was her sixth birthday and she said she couldn't believe it was her own little cottage. It has a thatched roof and it's so pretty. We play house in there, and our friends come, too. We tidy and dust – all the things housemaids do.

We each have a patch of garden, so we went to see that.

'The gardeners have kept it beautifully tidy while we were away,' said Lilibet. 'There's not a weed in sight. We must find them and thank them.'

We talked about what we'll grow this year. 'Flowers,' said Lilibet. 'Lots of flowers to cheer everyone's spirits. What about you, Margaret?'

'Potatoes,' I said. 'Then if potatoes are ever rationed, the family will have plenty.'

'That's a lovely idea,' she said. But she's growing flowers all the same.

It's too cold and frosty to think of gardening. More snow's coming, Papa says, so we can do lovely things instead, like building snowmen and playing snowballs.

## February 12th

Lilibet had a letter from Philip. He's being posted to a ship, but he's not allowed to say where. She was a little moody after she read the letter. I think it's because she knows she won't see him for ages.

'Maybe the war will be over in a few weeks, then he can come to stay,' I said.

She hugged me and said I'm the best sister ever. I'm the only one as far as she's concerned, so it's jolly good luck for her that I am the best!

## March 4th

Lilibet's happy today because she's had another letter from Philip.

'His ship can't be very comfortable,' she told me. 'It's so hot down below that the junior officers prefer to sleep in armchairs in the gunroom.'

'What's a gunroom?' I asked.

She shrugged. 'Where they keep guns, I suppose, though it doesn't seem likely.'

Later on, we asked Papa what a gunroom was. It's the junior officers' mess. A mess is not what it sounds like – it's where they dine and read and play cards and so on. Knowing boys, I expect it actually is a mess.

We played duets this afternoon on the piano. You could tell Lilibet was happy; she thumped away at the keys, and didn't mind at all when I made mistakes. She never actually says anything about my mistakes, but I can tell it's annoying.

## April 12th

'The beastly Germans have invaded Denmark,' Lilibet told me this afternoon. 'How sad for poor Philip.'

'It's sad for the Danish people,' I said, 'but why is it sad for Philip? He's probably nowhere near there.'

'Prince Philip of Greece and Denmark?'

'Oh,' I said, as the penny dropped. 'That's rotten, then.'

I did think it was strange that she told everyone she met about 'poor Philip'. She seems to think about him rather a lot. Mummy said he must come and stay when he's on leave.

That cheered Lilibet up no end. She doesn't get that excited when our other boy cousins are invited.

Then I heard that Hitler didn't just invade Denmark. He's invaded Norway and the Netherlands, too. Lilibet didn't mention them. She didn't mention any of our relations in those countries, either, but I bet she'll say a prayer for them tonight. Lilibet doesn't forget much.

Photographs in the gardens today. Jackets and skirts and jumpers, which aren't really garden-y, but Mummy likes us to be smart. Lilibet and I looked exactly alike, except I had socks on and she didn't. We posed and smiled, and crossed streams and did everything the photographer wanted. I was constantly in danger of getting my shoes and socks wet, because I have to charge across stepping stones instead of taking it steadily. Luckily, Lilibet's always there, ready to grab me when I wobble.

Afterwards we posed on a wall with Mummy and Papa. Jane and Dookie joined us, but no matter how hard Papa tried, they refused to look at the camera. Not everyone obeys the King!

## April 21st

Lilibet's birthday. She's fourteen – almost grown up. I don't like her getting older, because she doesn't like to play so much. I can't remember when we last groomed our little horses together. She does sit and chat sometimes, when I'm doing it. And she tells me if I'm doing it wrong.

'It doesn't matter if I do wrong,' I said the other evening.

'Yes, it does,' she said. 'You must always try to do things the right way, Margaret. Anyway, horses don't like being brushed in the wrong direction.'

'They haven't complained,' I said, and she laughed.

Today she's had hundreds of cards and telegrams and presents, including the usual two pearls from Papa, to add to those already on her necklace. When she's twenty-one, it will be complete.

I happened to notice (because I peeked) that one birthday card has made it to Lilibet's bedside drawer. It's easy to guess who that one's from. Philip! She gets embarrassed when I tease her about him, so I haven't mentioned the card. But I might.

There was one disappointment – no icing on the birthday cake, because sugar's rationed. But Lilibet said it doesn't matter, because icing's so sickly. She didn't think that last year when she saved her icing till I'd eaten mine, then ate hers very slowly, to make me jealous. But her little plan went wrong, because Crawfie gave me her icing, so I had mine last after all!

## April 22nd

I didn't say anything to Lilibet about her keeping Philip's card in her bedside drawer. I don't want to upset her. I'll remember it, though, in case I need to tease her!

## May 14th

We've moved again, but only three miles away, to Windsor Castle. Mummy says it's just for a while, maybe a week or so. I love looking out of the window and seeing people start out for a stroll at the far end of the Long Walk. I go away and do something, and when I come back they're still going. The walk is over two and a half miles long!

Everyone's talking about a speech Mr Winston Churchill, our new prime minister, made yesterday. It was about how all he has to offer are blood, toil, tears and sweat, and how we're aiming at victory. He says we'll win, however long and hard the road may be.

It doesn't look as if the war's going to finish any time soon.


## May 20th


Ten days ago, that awful Adolf Hitler invaded the Netherlands. Well, his armies did. He doesn't do any fighting himself.

The Queen of the Netherlands, Wilhelmina, has come to England. Papa met her at Liverpool Street station, and took her to stay at Buckingham Palace. It will be nice for her to have Mummy to talk to.

Lilibet said, 'Poor Queen Wilhelmina. How hateful it must be to see foreigners taking over your country.'

Then she went quiet. I wondered if she was imagining what it would be like if it happened to her, when she becomes queen. It made me think. When she's Queen Elizabeth, she'll have the same sorts of worries that Papa has. She'll have to read all those papers that come in red boxes every day. She'll have to have meetings with the prime minister. And she'll worry about our people all the time, like Mummy and Papa do. I don't think it's much fun ruling a country. I'd rather stay just a princess.

## June 5th

I hear planes going over at night. They always come just as I'm dropping off. They must be ours or the sirens would sound. It frightens me to know that a bomb could fall on the castle. The Germans did a huge bombing of Holland, Belgium and Luxembourg last month. Who'll be next?

If there's an air raid, and the sirens sound, we have to go down and down stairs, clutching our gas masks, to a part of the castle we've never been to before. It's a sort of dungeon below ground level, and the passages leading to it are damp and cold and smell disgusting. Did they really put prisoners down there? I would have died of misery. Imagine being locked up in the cold, damp darkness, away from your family and the sunshine. Horrible.

We take a small case down with us when we go, full of precious things we couldn't bear to lose if the castle was bombed. I bet prisoners weren't allowed a little case like that.

We have chairs, beds, food, books and everything we need in our dungeon. Prisoners had nothing to sit or sleep on but dirty, damp straw.

When we go down, I know Lilibet's as scared as me, but she never shows it, so I try to be like her. It's not easy.


## June 6th


Her Royal Highness Princess Elizabeth is extremely indignant! In fact, she's fuming!

What happened was the Lord Chancellor wrote to the prime minister saying that Lilibet and I should be sent to Canada. It was because the Nazis had tried desperately hard to capture the Dutch royal family. Mr Churchill told Mummy and Papa what the Lord Chancellor said, and Mummy told him absolutely no! She said Princess Elizabeth and Princess Margaret wouldn't leave the country without her. She would never leave the country without the King, and the King would never leave his people. It was as simple as that.

Lilibet couldn't believe anyone would think she'd leave England.

'He's thinking about our safety,' I said. 'He meant well. You ought to write and thank him, not get cross.'

'I don't think a letter is necessary,' said Mummy.

I was joking, actually.

Everyone's thinking about safety. Shooting ranges have been set up at Buckingham Palace and here at Windsor, so Mummy and Papa and other members of our households can learn to shoot. I expect the townspeople wonder what on earth is happening when they hear shots. Mind, they're used to odd goings-on in the park. There are aeroplanes parked on Smith's Lawn, near the airstrip, and servicemen camped there, too.

I imagined Mummy in her pretty clothes and pearl necklace, her hat laden with flowers and a gun in her hand. It's funny, but at the same time, it isn't. Not really.

## June 9th

I stayed up till nine last night to listen to a special *Bandwagon* programme. It hasn't been on for months. Arthur Askey and Richard Murdoch made me giggle, but sometimes the others laughed at bits that didn't seem funny to me. There was a singer called Dolly Elsie, and once I'd caught on to the tunes, I joined in. Papa said I was marvellous, but I don't think Mummy and Lilibet were quite as pleased. My sister likes to listen to the wireless properly, without missing a word.

Once I was tucked up in bed, I started to worry. I don't know why. I thought about the hateful Nazis and how beastly to try to capture Queen Wilhelmina's family. Suppose they captured us? They might demand a ransom before they'd let us go. Suppose they said to Mr Churchill, 'If you don't surrender to Germany, we'll kill your royal family.' Suppose they said that?

I went to my sister, and snuggled in beside her.

'What's wrong, Margaret?' she said. 'You woke me from a lovely dream.'

'I'm frightened.' I told her what was scaring me.

After a moment, she said, 'What a dreadful thought. Imagine, the British nation ending up being ruled by Hitler, simply to save our lives.'

'They might not, Lilibet,' I said. 'The government might say, "We'll never surrender to you, you horrible bully." What would happen then?'

'Then,' said Lilibet, 'we'd have to be braver than we ever imagined in our lives.' She stroked my forehead. 'But Margaret, it won't happen, you know. Mummy and Papa are guarded constantly, and you and I are safe here in the castle. We're a secret, did you know?'

'A secret?'

She nodded. 'Nobody is to know we're here.'

'But hundreds of people know we're here,' I said. 'The staff, the guards, our friends, our family, our music and French teachers…'

'They're all loyal to Britain,' said Lilibet. 'It's the newspapers and the wireless who are keeping quiet about where we are, so no German spies read or hear about us. All they say is that we're "somewhere in the country". It's all for the good, so nothing can happen to us. You mustn't worry. Come on, I'll take you back to bed.'

As she tucked me in, she said, 'Anyway, who'd want to kidnap a cheeky monkey like you? You're not the queen, and you're not the heir to the throne. You'd be more trouble than you're worth!' She kissed me good night.

I thought about what Lilibet said. It's true. I'm not important, not the heir to the throne.

But she is.


## June 10th


Italy's declared war on us now! Everything's getting worse.

It's Prince Philip's birthday today, and Lilibet's fretting about whether or not he's received the birthday card and letter she sent.

I'm fretting about my sister. We cycle in the gardens sometimes, and we're often completely out of sight of anyone at all. I keep imagining a horrid Nazi hiding in the bushes, waiting to kidnap her. Then a nasty ransom note, saying, 'People of Britain, we have the heir to the throne. Surrender now or it'll be the worse for her,' or something like that. I'm afraid to let Lilibet out of my sight. If it happened, at least I could scream and shout and bring the guardsmen running.

I imagined how proud everyone would be. 'Gosh,' they'd say, 'Princess Margaret's not even ten, and she's saved the life of the heir to the throne.' Then I imagined someone saying, 'The amazing girl's done more than that – she's saved Britain from the Nazis – singlehanded!'

Suddenly I noticed Lilibet staring at me oddly.

'Margaret Rose, you are a funny little thing! Why on earth are you talking to yourself and making such strange faces?'

I burst out laughing and ran to hug her. 'Come on,' I said. 'Let's go and groom our horses.'

She followed me upstairs, but I think she's too old for toy horses now. All she did was talk about Philip and wonder what it was like to spend your birthday on a warship. He's probably having a party.

# July 15th

There are terrible air raids night after night. Papa told his secretary (I was listening) that this is the battle for Britain. It started with lots of small aeroplanes trying to shoot each other down over the English Channel, between us and France. The Germans are so close.

Our grandmother, Queen Mary, has gone to live in Badminton House, in Gloucestershire. She's an evacuee! Lilibet and I think she's sensible to leave London, because when you're older you can't run so fast during an air raid.

Last week, Mummy took us to London for the day, so we could see that everything's still all right at Buckingham Palace. The garden looked different, because the gardeners have dug up great chunks of it to grow vegetables.

There's a special room where Papa and Mummy go during air raids. It's a housemaids' sitting room that's been made very strong with wood and steel. It's plain, but Mummy says it's perfectly serviceable. Better than our dungeons, anyway. I hope it keeps them safe.

# July 18th

I overheard something today and I wish I hadn't, because it put ghastly pictures in my mind. I told Lilibet, and she said I shouldn't snoop. I really don't, but when I hear people saying interesting things, well, naturally, I listen.

I heard that Papa was visiting a village, and a few minutes after he left – minutes – the village was bombed. Did the Nazis know he'd be there? Are they spying on him?

It hasn't put off my brave papa, or Mummy. They've been touring towns that have been bombed, and visiting the poor people who have lost their houses. Mummy always wears something pretty and bright, because she hopes it will cheer the people up. You need a lot of cheering up if you haven't got a house to live in.

I can't get it out of my head that the Nazis are watching Papa, and that if they're watching the King, they might be watching the girl who'll be the next queen. My sister, Elizabeth.

Well, I'll watch Lilibet, too. I'll keep my eyes peeled whenever we're out. If anyone's watching her, I'll see them first. The trouble is that I don't know how to tell someone is a spy, unless he speaks.

## August 15th

There are German planes everywhere. We're not allowed to leave the castle, just in case.

## August 17th

The south-west of London was badly bombed yesterday. It was Friday, so lots of people were at work. It must have been just terrible. Lilibet said she's heard that one of our kitchen maids went home because her mother was ill, and found no house at all – just a pile of brick, wood, broken glass and a bath. Luckily her mother's in hospital.

## September 8th

There's bombing all the time. I hate it. I'm frightened for Mummy and Papa. Every day they're either out visiting, or they're in the palace. I'm so afraid a bomber will fly over London, see our home and bomb it. Every time Mummy and Papa are due back at Windsor, I can't bear the wait until they appear.

But I never tell them how worried I am. Lilibet told me I can do my bit by keeping my chin up, so I'm trying, but it doesn't exactly help the war effort! She says as soon as she's old enough she'll join up and become a lady soldier or something. 'That's how I want to do my bit for the war effort,' she said, 'but don't tell anyone, Margaret.'

Granny won't like that.

Everyone's doing their bit except me. I can't do anything. I haven't got a bit to do.

We hear the bombs sometimes. Crawfie does her best to ignore them, but I think even she is nervous. The maids are. I hear them talking. They're really scared, but they keep going, so we must, too.

## September 12th

Lilibet was quiet this morning. She didn't want to say what was wrong, but I made her.

'You mustn't worry, Margaret,' she said. 'What's happened has happened, and everyone's all right.'

'What was it?' I asked. 'Tell me, or I'll imagine something even worse. I'll have bad dreams, you know I will.'

She smiled. 'Your dreams are exciting, not bad,' she said. 'Not that I believe half of them.'

I grinned. 'Tell me!'

I stopped smiling when she told me that a bomb had fallen on our terrace at Buckingham Palace. It didn't blow up straight away, but it exploded later on and blew out windows and smashed the conservatory.

'Our swimming pool was blown up, too,' said Lilibet.

'They'll mend it, won't they?' I asked.

She was shocked. 'You mustn't think of things like that when people are fighting for their lives, Margaret.'

I folded my arms and stuck my lip out. 'I was actually thinking about it being mended after the war,' I said, which wasn't strictly true.

# September 16th

I noticed that Mummy and Papa are quieter than usual. Mummy's pale and wants to rest a lot. It's only today that I've found out what happened when the palace was bombed.

Lilibet and I are truly upset. I hate the Nazis, hate them, hate them, hate them. We're not sure exactly what happened, because our parents have only told us bits, but we've managed to piece it together.

A German bomber flew straight up the Mall and dropped six bombs on Buckingham Palace. Mummy and Papa were sitting together in the maids' room, and one of the bombs blew out their windows. They were covered in broken glass. I can't bear it. Another bomb ruined the chapel, but we haven't found out what the others have done.

We begged Mummy and Papa to stay in Windsor, but they say they've their duty to do, however difficult. The people have to keep calm and carry on as usual. So will they.

Lilibet tried to explain how important duty is, but it doesn't help to know all that stuff when your parents have been practically blown up.

'They weren't anywhere near being blown up,' said Lilibet.

'That afternoon they visited the East End of London. It's far worse there.'

No one's to know how close they came to disaster, so we mustn't write about it to anybody. Lilibet said she won't tell Philip. I wonder.

No, if she says she won't, she won't. She does her duty.

### September 24th

Something so thrilling is happening. My sister's going to talk on the wireless. Princess Elizabeth on *Children's Hour*!

'Are you excited?' I asked.

She made a face – not the sort of face I pull, but a mouth-turned-down one. 'I'm nervous,' she said.

'It'll be fine,' I said. 'You'll read your speech. You won't have to learn it like we have to learn all that poetry with Crawfie.' I do struggle with learning by heart. Except songs. I learn music and songs as quickly as anything.

## October 1st

A German Messerschmitt aeroplane crashed in the park! It's been screened off and they're charging sixpence to see it. The money's going to a fund for our Hurricane fighter aeroplanes, so that's a splendid idea. Crawfie took us to see it, and they let us in free. The cockpit's tiny. I could never sit in there. I hate being in small spaces. When I saw the mess it was in I was surprised the pilot wasn't killed. He was captured, though, by a Hurricane pilot!

Not enough German planes have crashed, because it's been bombs bombs bombs, raids raids raids, night after night and even in daytime.

## October 8th

It's really irritating. Lilibet has to go off and practise her speech, and learn to use a microphone, all without me. It's bad enough that she has some of her lessons without me, too. She has special history ones with a teacher called Mr Marten from Eton College. Actually, it's not exciting history, like about Queen Elizabeth and the Spanish Armada, or King Henry VIII and his wives. It's called constitutional history, and sounds deadly dull. It's stuff she needs to know for when she's queen. She says it's interesting, but she would say that. If it was me I'd be gazing out of the window humming dance tunes, but Lilibet's very good at concentrating.

She was revising French today, when Crawfie left the room. After a minute or two I looked up. She was staring into space.

'What are you daydreaming about?' I asked.

She smiled. 'I was wondering if Philip might hear my speech next week.'

I laughed. 'Don't be silly. He's at sea!'

She looked cross. 'My broadcast is to all the children of the British Empire,' she said. 'He might be somewhere where he can hear it.'

I giggled. 'He might, but I doubt if the ship's captain will make everyone stop work for *Children's Hour*, just for Philip!'

She giggled, too, just as Crawfie came in and said, 'How are those French verbs coming along, Elizabeth? Are they amusing you?'

Lilibet and I spluttered with laughter, and in the end, even Crawfie laughed, though she didn't have a clue what she was laughing at.

# October 14th

My sister, Elizabeth, has been on the wireless, and SO HAVE I!!!

I sat beside her while she did her speech. First the announcer said, 'This is one of the most important days in the history of *Children's Hour*', then he introduced her.

I've heard Lilibet practise her speech so many times with Mummy that I must know it by heart. She told the children who've been evacuated that we understand how awful it is to be away from people you love. That's true, because our parents have to go away on long overseas visits. Lilibet said everything would turn out all right and then, just at the end, she said, 'My sister is by my side, and we are both going to say good night to you. Come on, Margaret.'

And then I was allowed to say, 'Good night, children!'

Lilibet finished by saying, 'Good night, and good luck to you all.'

Afterwards we said how strange it is that thousands and thousands of children could hear us. Papa said grown-ups would listen, too. Imagine all those people stopping whatever they were doing to listen to us. Well, to Lilibet. So exciting!

## October 24th

A noisy night, up and down to the dungeon shelters. Some bombs landed in Windsor yesterday evening, and then more at about half past five this morning. We hate going down below, but it's for our safety. Lilibet said it's better than going down into the tube stations, which is what Londoners have to do. I saw mice on the rails when we visited the underground. Imagine sleeping down there with creatures crawling over you. Ugh!

## November 2nd

My sister made me laugh until I cried today. Her tutor, Mr Marten, usually cycles from Eton College to the castle for her lessons, but sometimes, like today, she goes to his study.

Lilibet imitated him sucking his handkerchief, leaning back to stare into space and knocking piles of books over. She says there's a pet raven in his study, which I can't believe. She keeps an eye on it in case it perches on the back of her chair and pecks her ear. It's so unusual to see Lilibet doing silly things, and she was so funny. She should be silly more often!

In return, I pretended to be the housemaid, flat on the floor, stretching under my bed to reach the slipper I'd kicked beneath it. Her legs go up and down like scissors and she grunts like a pig.

I love watching people. Once Mummy entertained a very elderly guest to tea. His nose was screwed up as if he'd smelt something nasty, and his lips twitched in one corner. As I offered cake, I made sure he couldn't see me, and I wrinkled my nose and twitched like mad. Lilibet actually giggled, and Mummy had an awful time trying not to laugh. I sort of got into trouble for that, but Papa said I'm his little ray of sunshine, and I keep everyone cheery and that's worth gold in wartime. I mustn't do it again, though, he said.

Keeping people cheerful isn't as good as joining up, but it's something.

Greece is in the war now. Philip told Lilibet all about it in his latest letter. She writes back straight away. I hate it when people do that, because it means you have to start another letter so soon after the one you've just sent.

# November 16th

Papa has rushed to Coventry. The whole city's been terribly badly bombed. Six hundred people were killed. Alla says it gave the poor Londoners a break from the bombing that's been going on night after night, though that seems to have stopped now.

'Wouldn't it be wonderful if the war ended tomorrow,' I said to Lilibet. 'Everything would go back to normal.'

'If only it could,' she said, 'then all our soldiers, sailors and airmen could come home safely.'

I know which sailor she was thinking about. Prince Philip! She mentions him whenever she can. At breakfast, she's always saying, 'Philip says this, and Philip says that.'

'I think you're sweet on him,' I whispered one day when we were making Christmas cards. 'Don't be stupid,' she said. 'You don't know what you're talking about. What does "sweet on him" mean, anyway?'

I made a kissy noise, and she turned the colour of raspberry juice, I swear she did!

We've been warned that Christmas won't be like our normal Christmases. Nothing's normal. There's that horrid blackout, and the rooms don't look the same. The pictures have been taken away to be stored safely. Lilibet and I quite liked all those portraits looking down on us. Empty frames make the walls look dreary. All the china and glass has been safely stored. The glittering chandeliers have gone, too. Mummy says they'd cost a fortune to replace if they were smashed.

Everywhere's gloomy. Even the light bulbs in our bedrooms are gloomy.


## December 18th


I must stop teasing Lilibet about Philip. I got sent from the dining table to my room the other day for singing 'Elizabeth and Philip sitting in a tree, K-I-S-S-I-N-G'. It was a bad time to do it, as we had some Guards officers for lunch. Not for lunch, to lunch.

Poor Lilibet. She hoped Philip might visit us over Christmas and he isn't going to. She's down in the dumps today. I hope she gets another letter before Christmas to cheer her up.

Mummy and Papa are spending lots of time with us. We've played them all the piano tunes we've been practising, and sung some French duets and I've recited some funny poems with all the voices. I think Mummy's a bit tired of listening to us, but Papa keeps smiling.

I sing solos to them, too. They say I've a lovely voice, even better than Lilibet's, which is very nice. That reminded me about the singing lessons I want, so I asked again.

Papa laughed. 'Certainly not!' And he wouldn't budge.

That surprised me! Even if he says no, I can usually wheedle and get him to change his mind. This time he was definite.

Lilibet asked, 'Why can't she, Papa? I have my history lessons. It would be nice for Margaret to have something special for herself.'

Papa ruffled my hair. 'Singing lessons are a waste of time.'

'They're not!' said Mummy and Lilibet together.

'They are!' he said. 'And I'll tell you how I know. Your Aunt Mary, the Princess Royal, had many singing lessons, and they did her no good at all. She makes the most ghastly racket in church.'

That's interesting. I'll listen for her next time we're all at a wedding or some other service. I'll copy her, so there's two of us making a ghastly racket. What fun!

# December 22nd

Lilibet got a letter! She's walking round with the biggest smile and is sweet to everybody. I think if I asked her right now to give me anything of hers that I wanted, I'd get it. But I wouldn't be so mean. Or would I? Hee hee!

Philip wrote a jolly note to me, too, and sent some jokes that I'm trying to learn. He's going to Malta, Lilibet says, though he doesn't say that in his letters. 'You mustn't tell a soul,' she said. 'If the enemy were to find out...'

I don't think the enemy are likely to find out from me where Philip is, and I shouldn't think they'd care much if they did. They wouldn't bother holding him to ransom. His family have no money, and they don't even have a country. In the 1920s his father was banished from Greece for life.

'How do you know where he is?' I asked.

She gave a sly smile. 'Haven't you heard of secret codes?'

I don't believe her. Papa must have told her. Philip's in the Royal Navy, and if it's royal then the King can find out anything he wants.

# January 11th 1941

The first letter Lilibet had this year hasn't exactly cheered her up. Philip is still far away, visiting relations in Greece. He thinks they're all going to leave there soon.

'Papa told Philip he may visit whenever he's able,' Lilibet said, 'and he's promised to come when he's next in London. It'll be lovely to see him again.'

I grinned. 'I bet you can't wait!'

I hope it's soon. He's rather a jolly type.

# March 3rd

Lilibet didn't open all her letters today, I noticed. She tucked one in her pocket, and slipped away as soon as we were free of Crawfie. I followed, but I couldn't find her. She must have found a place where she can be private. My fault, I expect, because I do tease her.

She couldn't keep quiet for long, though. She was obviously bursting to tell someone about her letter.

'Philip's having a splendid time in Greece,' she said. 'He's visited the King, and his cousin Crown Prince Paul. They've enjoyed themselves in spite of the war; there are lots of parties, and they actually go up on the palace roof to watch the air raids.'

'How brave!' I said.

'How stupid!' said Lilibet. 'He might get killed.'

She must wish she was there, I thought. Then I realised, no, she wishes he was here. She likes him a lot. A lot. Poor Lilibet.

## April 4th

Papa told Lilibet a secret. She asked if she could tell me, and he said yes. He's heard that Philip was very brave and did so well in battle that he was 'mentioned in dispatches'. That doesn't sound too exciting, but Lilibet said it's a very good thing. She said it in such an important way that I feel I ought to use capitals. A Very Good Thing.

'And, Margaret, guess what!' she went on. 'He's coming back to England to sit some exams to become a sub-lieutenant!'

Without thinking, I told Crawfie about Philip being brave, and she said something to Lilibet, who came to me and said, 'You shouldn't have told anyone. I won't tell you any more secrets.'

She will. She can't help it.

## April 19th

We had our photos taken, digging in our gardens, to show that we royals are Digging for Victory. As Lilibet and I posed, I sang quietly, 'Dig, dig, dig, and your muscles will grow big,' and Lilibet laughed so much her foot slipped off her spade!

'One more, please, Ma'am?' said the poor photographer.

No one will believe we were really digging, because of the clothes we wore. Alla says we must always be properly turned out when we're in public, but why do we always have to dress as if we're visiting an art gallery?

Papa says the moat at the Tower of London has been dug up, and is full of vegetables!

# April 26th

We've spent a week dressing some of our dolls. They'll be auctioned to raise money. I've never pricked my poor fingers so much. Alla, Crawfie, Bobo and Ruby all joined in, and Mummy supervised. The dolls looked lovely in the end, but I never want to see them again. One gentleman said we were good, generous girls to give our dolls away, but I never really liked them.

Some kind people sent Lilibet and me a model of a Spitfire aeroplane. It's so clever, because it's made out of bits of a German Dornier bomber that was shot down. When I heard that, I said, 'We can't have a German bomber on our mantelpiece,' and I took it down. But Lilibet put it straight back.

'The Spitfire will remind us of the dangerous work our airmen do,' she said, 'and because it's made out of a German bomber, it will remind us that there's one fewer load of bombs to destroy our cities.'

She's right. She always is, which is annoying. It's because she thinks before she speaks, which I don't do very much.

# May 4th

Philip has been to visit. Lilibet was so excited when she heard he was coming. Papa swears Philip's grown. He's suntanned, and his hair's fairer than ever. And he's grown a little beard. My sister thinks it makes him look distinguished, but I heard Papa mutter, 'Scruffy'.

Papa took Philip fishing, and we all had some great horse rides together. Philip made us laugh a lot at dinner with some of his stories about ship life. Mummy tutted quite a bit, but even she couldn't help laughing, because he's so noisy and funny. I can see why Lilibet likes him. I do, too, but he doesn't make me go pink.

After dinner each evening, we played very noisy card games of things like racing demon. Mummy says I get over-excited and start squeaking, but you should see Philip! He loves to win!

He totted up the scores at the end of each game. He almost always won, and Crawfie thinks his arithmetic needs some attention.

Now he's gone, but he's left something behind. Lilibet doesn't know I know, but I do. He left a photograph of himself. I bet he's gone away with one of HRH Princess Elizabeth!

Lilibet really enjoyed his visit, and so did I.

## July 23rd

Mummy and Papa held a dance here at the castle and as I'm nearly eleven, I was allowed to go!

We put on a concert the day before to raise money to buy wool. Lilibet and I were both in it and I absolutely adored it. We sang and danced, and did our French duets, which some people said was very clever. We played the piano. We bowed and were applauded. At the very end, we did Mr Churchill's 'V' for victory sign. That made everybody cheer!

What the audience didn't know (but I told them afterwards) was that Lilibet and I helped design and paint the scenery. That was fun! I've only ever painted on paper before with small brushes, but this time we used huge brushes to paint big areas. I got in such a mess. It was glorious.

The dance was ace, as Ruby says, because there was a wonderful band, led by a man called Jack Jackson. They played all the latest tunes as well as what they call 'old favourites', and kept going for hours and hours.

So did I! I stayed right to the very end. Mummy kept suggesting it was time to go upstairs, but I begged her to let me stay. I danced with Papa, and with Mr Tanner, the headmaster of the Royal School in Windsor, and Papa's secretary and equerry, and with all sorts of people I didn't even know! It was all so jolly. Lilibet danced practically every dance, and we all ended up doing the conga, which Papa started!

I wonder if Lilibet wished she was dancing with Philip. I bet she did! Dare I ask her?

## July 27th

We had a lovely cycle ride through the Great Park with Crawfie, and a huge picnic back in the Home Park. It's odd to see anti-aircraft guns so close by. I said, 'I hope they don't blow a chunk off the castle,' and Crawfie told me that the guns have been specially fixed so they can't fire that low. That's a relief!

People waved to us, but they didn't come over. Crawfie said that was very considerate.

While we were eating, Crawfie asked why I kept fidgeting.

'I don't know,' I said, and I didn't. But later, I realised I was fidgety because I felt uneasy. There we were, surrounded by acres of land and hundreds of trees. There could have been a spy behind any one of them, waiting for a chance to kidnap the heir to the British throne. I didn't say, of course, because I wouldn't worry Lilibet for anything. But I kept my eyes peeled.

When I mentioned that there aren't as many deer around as there used to be, Lilibet said, 'They had to use them because of the evacuees – all those extra mouths to feed.'

How awful. Those beautiful deer. Lilibet said the evacuees must eat something, and if we had food they could use, then we should let them have it.

'I bet they don't eat deer in London, out of newspaper.'

Lilibet became all big sister-ish then, and said, 'Margaret Rose! Don't be unkind. Think yourself lucky that we've everything we need, while most people have to do without.'

I could do without being told off for nothing. She's fifteen, not a grown-up.


## September 3rd


Mummy and Papa have come up to Balmoral as often as possible, and we've been having a lovely summer with

Crawfie and Alla and everyone. We feel safe here, though I never forget there could be a Nazi hiding behind every pine tree. Well, not really, they'd have to find trees with thicker trunks. But when we're out riding, I'm suspicious every time I see a stag. I keep wondering, is it a stag? Or a pair of antlers tied on top of a German head?

I know all the grown-ups were taught to shoot, but Crawfie doesn't carry a gun, and nor do the men who ride out with us. Not that I can see, anyway.

## September 8th

Crawfie has had the most wonderful idea. She thinks we could put on a pantomime, for people to watch, and pay money!

'What a wizard idea!' I said.

'Margaret,' said Lilibet, 'don't use slang.'

She's so proper. But even she was excited. 'When could we begin, Crawfie?' she asked.

'Slow down,' said Crawfie, laughing. 'I must ask the King and Queen first.'

'Oh, they'll say yes, I'm sure,' cried Lilibet. 'Especially as it's for a good cause.'

'Then, with luck,' said Crawfie, 'when we get back to Windsor…'

'Hooray!' we cheered.

## September 15th

It's rather chilly at the moment – we're in kilts and thick jumpers most of the time.

Lilibet twitches every time the telephone rings. I know why! It's because Philip is in London visiting Greek relations. The Greek king is living in a hotel, and Philip's staying at a house in Chester Street that belongs to Uncle Dickie, who is actually Philip's own uncle!

Uncle Dickie's real name is Louis, and he's the son of Prince Louis of Battenberg. Papa gets on well with him. Mummy is always lovely to him, because she's lovely to everyone, but I don't think he's her favourite relation. Not at all.

## October 18th

I'm sure Lilibet would pine away if we let her. Philip has telephoned but she hasn't seen him yet, even though we're back home. He's met Granny, and she wrote to Papa and Mummy that he's a very bright young man. She doesn't say that about everyone!

Papa told Lilibet what Granny had said, and she went pink and smiled that enormous smile she gives when she's really happy. She must have a huge crush on Philip.

## October 29th

The pantomime's under way and some of the cast have been chosen. Lilibet and I will have the main parts, of course. (Crawfie said there's no 'of course' about it, but that didn't make any difference.)

Philip has been visiting our uncle and aunt at their home, Coppins, in Buckinghamshire. Uncle George and

Aunt Marina have a boy called Edward, and a dear little girl called Alexandra. She'll be five on Christmas Day, and she's so sweet. Everybody loves her. Edward and Alexandra are our cousins, and I suppose they're also Philip's cousins, because he is cousin to Aunt Marina, who is a princess of Greece. We royal families are so complicated!

Papa just sent a message that we are to go to Buckingham Palace in a day or two. We haven't been for ages. Lilibet's excited, I can tell, and that's not like her at all. She loves the country more than town. She's always wanted a nice country house with lots of horses, dogs and children. Now she's itching to get back to London.

'The trees will be turning red, yellow and gold,' she said. 'London's so beautiful at this time of year. It will be lovely to see it.'

I know what she's hoping. And I hope we'll see Philip, too.

Gosh! I think she's already sorting out the things she's taking with her!

## November 3rd

Philip was a guest at lunch today. Goodness, that young man eats well! Perhaps the food on board ship isn't very nice, so he's making up for it. He entertained Papa with tales of life at sea afterwards. Of course, Papa knows all about that, because he's been in the navy, too.

Afterwards, Lilibet, Philip and I went for a walk in the gardens. I don't think Lilibet took much notice of the lovely autumn leaves!

As we sat by the lake, Philip said, 'You'll be queen, one day, Elizabeth. Do you have time to do the sort of things you like, or are you always studying and learning about what you're going to have to do?'

'I do have to study different things from Margaret,' said Lilibet, 'but I still have time to myself. And I learn an awful lot just by watching the King and Queen.'

Philip nodded. 'Yes, they're jolly good sorts, aren't they?'

'I'll say!' I said, flicking bits of twig into the water. 'Britain's very lucky to have them.'

'And they're very lucky to have Britain,' said Lilibet.

I don't know why, but when she says that sort of thing, I feel she's putting me in my place. I told Crawfie that once, and she said, 'No, dear, she's not. Lilibet is simply extremely serious about these things.'

Duty again, I suppose.

Anyway, we had a smashing afternoon, and we'd all worked up a huge appetite by tea time!

Mummy told Philip about the pantomime we're going to put on at Windsor. It's to raise money, of course, but we'll invite troops to watch, and Lilibet thinks they shouldn't have to pay, as they're giving so much to their country already. She said to Philip. 'If you're in England at Christmas time, perhaps you'd...'

'Come and see the two jolliest girls in Windsor doing their stuff on the stage?' he said, grinning. 'If I could, I would.'

That wasn't quite the answer Lilibet wanted, I could see, so I said, 'Oh do! I'm Cinderella and Elizabeth is Prince Charming.' Then I had a bright idea. 'Philip,' I said, 'wouldn't it be a good idea if you were to teach her how to be a charming prince?'

Everyone burst out laughing, which wasn't what I'd expected. But I did see Lilibet turn bright pink. Serves her right for laughing at me.

## December 5th

Things are getting dreadfully serious; the country must be short of soldiers. Women aged between twenty and thirty are being called up to serve in the war. They don't have to be soldiers or sailors. They can join other things, like the fire brigade, or the police. And girls aged sixteen and over are having to register their names. I suppose that's so the government will know when they're twenty.

Golly, do they really think the war will last that long? How gloomy. And I feel even gloomier when I realise that my sister will be sixteen next birthday.

Oh, come on, Margaret! (That's me giving myself a good shake.) They'd never put the future queen in the army, would they?

I'm off to rehearsal now. Look out, everyone, here comes Cinders!


## December 6th


Rehearsal was such fun! We don't have costumes yet, and that's what makes it all so silly that we kept collapsing with laughter. Princess Elizabeth, in a sensible skirt and jumper and her comfy brown shoes, strutting about the stage pretending to be a prince! I love doing my part, sweeping and dusting, and crying when my ugly sisters are beastly to me.

We're doing it in the huge Waterloo Chamber, which will soon have a stage. There'll be wonderful costumes, but they're being hired, so we haven't seen them yet. I can't wait. I adore dressing up.

Mr Tanner, the local schoolmaster, brings some of his schoolchildren, and they'll all be in the pantomime with us. Most of them came today. They were terribly shy at first, and so were we. Well, I wasn't actually, but Lilibet hung back, so I thought I should. Whenever we're in public, it's always useful to watch her to see what to do. She never does it wrong.

Mummy went to speak to the children, and Lilibet followed, so I did, too. Once they got used to us, and to being in the castle, we were soon all laughing and chatting. I loved being with them. Some of them asked me questions, and I asked them questions, too, about their school, and the games they play. They've learned all their lines, but so have we.

Papa refused to let us have one of the carriages indoors, but we've found a spiffing replacement to take me to the ball. It's Queen Anne's sedan chair! And we're going to fill the empty picture frames with pantomime posters, to brighten the room. An evacuee called Claude is painting them on rolls of wallpaper. I can't wait to see them!

## December 9th

Nobody's enthusiastic about rehearsals today, even though it's not long till our first performance. Everybody's glued to the news.

The American navy had a fleet of ships in a place called Pearl Harbor, in Hawaii, in the Pacific Ocean. Two days ago, over three hundred Japanese planes bombed and torpedoed the ships. 'Sitting ducks, poor souls,' is how one of the maids described it. Thousands of sailors were killed and over a thousand more wounded.

Just when I begin to feel there's hope the war might end, this happens. It's too awful. Lilibet said, 'Imagine, Margaret, thousands of families are mourning their loved ones.'

And just before Christmas. It couldn't be more beastly.

## December 12th

One good thing (for us) has come out of the attack on Pearl Harbor. The Americans have joined the war – on our side, of course. We are allies.

## December 15th

Our costumes are gorgeous! I have a powdered wig, except it's not actually powdered – it just looks as if it is. My final dress is a perfectly beautiful embroidered gown with lace flounces on the sleeves, and pink roses, and I have pretend jewels and a fan.

Lilibet looks super. She has a satin jacket that comes to the top of her legs, and shiny breeches that just cover her knees. Then there are long, tight boots up to her knees.

We're having a chorus of Grenadier Guards, and their bandsmen will be our orchestra. What fun to do things together! How talented we all are!

## December 16th

The bright Lilibet smile looks as if it's stuck on her face with spirit gum, because Philip is coming to the pantomime. He said that our invitation was a royal command, so he had no choice. I thought that was a bit insulting, but Lilibet said it was a joke.

'He has such a jolly sense of humour, Margaret. You mustn't be offended. He doesn't mean to be rude; it's just the way his jokes come out.'

'He'd better be careful how he tells his jokes in front of the rest of the family,' I said.

## December 18th

I felt too sick to get up this morning, but I had to. Mummy said it's nerves. It's dress-rehearsal day, and lots of the household and some elderly people from the village are coming to watch.

'Suppose I forget my lines?' I groaned.

'Don't worry, Margaret,' said Lilibet. 'If you did, I'd whisper to you.'

'What if you're not on stage?' I wailed.

'Then I'll hiss from behind the scenery,' she said. 'If you forget, move to the back, and I'll be there.'

She will, too.

# December 23rd

It's all over. Lilibet and I feel so flat. We did all our performances, and I never once forgot my lines. Yippee! Oh, I should so love to be an actress when I grow up. Or a singer. Or even a concert pianist. No, maybe not that. I'd be wanting to burst into song!

Mummy and Papa said we were both amazingly good. And my sister is walking on air!

'Guess what Philip said, Margaret,' she whispered. 'He said, "You were the finest Prince Charming I've ever seen, Lilibet, but far too pretty to play a boy."'

I was surprised at that. Not that he thinks she's pretty – she is. I was surprised that he calls her Lilibet. That boy does exactly as he pleases and I'm not sure I like it. He's not family, after all. Well, not proper close family, like we four. But Lilibet doesn't mind at all!

## December 24th

Poor Papa must do his Christmas message on the wireless tomorrow. I know he gets terribly agitated, and worries that he'll stammer. Mummy just says, 'You'll be fine, Bertie. Mr Logue has faith in you, and so have I.'

She'll be right. She usually is. Papa's going to talk about how the nation is one great family. That's a lovely thing, isn't it, to think of all of us as a family. I'm glad we don't all live together, though.

## January 10th 1942

It's so cold that even my bath water didn't seem particularly warm this morning. The bathroom was freezing, and when you only have five inches of water to sit in, it's best to wash quickly and get dried as soon as possible. Papa had black lines painted around all the baths, so everyone knows how much five inches is.

## February 11th

We had a long walk this morning. Wherever we go, there's always a policeman not far away, watching over us. I've almost stopped looking for Nazi spies behind trees and walls. Almost, but not quite. Before the war we were perfectly safe wandering around the Home Park, or cycling, but we have to take more care these days.

The Great Park looks strange. Huge areas have been ploughed up for growing crops. It's all to help the war effort.

'Everyone seems to help the war effort except us,' Lilibet grumbled. We'd just been chasing naughty Dookie, who'd run away, and we were wandering slowly back to Crawfie.

'We do help,' I said. 'We collect tinfoil.' Not that we come across much of that, but the kitchen and household staff collect for us. 'We raise money for wool, and we knit things.' Actually, knitting's not my favourite activity. I'd much sooner give concerts and charge people to come and watch me!

'As soon as I'm old enough,' Lilibet said, 'I'll ask Papa to let me do real service. He will, I'm sure.' She broke into a run. 'Come on, dogs!'

I don't think he'll let her.

## March 14th

Hooray! We're starting up Guides and Brownies again, here at Windsor! We'll have camps in the Home Park, and fires, and cook sausages, and go tracking in the woods. And OH! I am old enough to leave Brownies and become a Guide!

## April 14th

It's official. I'm now a Girl Guide, like Lilibet! We have a really nice company, with girls from the village, and some of the evacuees who were Guides in London. It's going to be such fun, except for one thing. We're not allowed to camp out overnight. I made a fuss about that, but Mummy just eyed me sternly and said, 'Margaret! Air raids?'

'Oh,' I said. I hadn't thought. Imagine being in a tent when the air-raid siren sounds.

Lilibet promised that we'll still have camps and fires and

we'll cook and wash up, and we can still have tents. We just can't be out after dark.

Mummy's off on a trip tomorrow. She visits factories, and talks to the women workers, cheering them up and telling them what a good job they're doing. I said to Lilibet, 'Will you ask Papa if you can work in a factory?'

She said, 'Don't be silly. I'll ask him if I can be a nurse, and go and work in the East End.'

'Why not ask to be a Land Girl?' I said. 'Then you could work here at Windsor.'

'I don't think so.'

## April 24th

My sister's been made Colonel of the Grenadier Guards, and on her birthday she made her first inspection. She held her first royal audience the day before, when the Lieutenant Colonel of the Guards came to talk about the ceremony, and what would happen.

On the day, Lilibet looked smart and grown-up in her blue-grey suit (blue suits us both), with the gold regimental badge pinned to her hat. Before we got out of the car, she said, 'Now, Margaret, when Papa salutes the officers, you must not salute.'

'As if I would!' I said.

'You used to,' she said. 'It was so embarrassing.'

'I was little then,' I began, but Mummy put a finger to her lips, and whispered to me, 'Lilibet's nervous, so forgive her for being snappy.'

Lilibet might have been nervous, but no one would ever have known, because she looked so calm. It was funny to see my sister lead the inspection, with Mummy and Papa following, instead of the other way around. Me? Trailing along behind, of course. But I was so proud, because my sister did it beautifully.

It must be weird for the Guardsmen, having a sixteen-year-old girl walk up and down their lines, inspecting them. I wonder what she'd do if she found a bit of fluff on a sleeve, or something! She never would, I'm sure, because they spend hours making their uniforms perfect.

They wouldn't think her so grand and ladylike if they could see her freewheeling down the hill on her bicycle with her legs stuck out, crying, 'Wheee!'

I'm not sure I like Lilibet being grown up. She's having her own suite of rooms, which means we won't be together all the time. Even worse, she's having ladies-in-waiting. It's their job to go with her (instead of me) on official engagements.

And what about poor Princess Margaret? Everything's still the same for me. I want to be grown up, too. I hate this boring war.

# Later


At tea time, Lilibet spoke to Crawfie about what to wear tomorrow. 'My Guide uniform, I think,' she said.

'What?' I said. 'Where are you going?'

'To the labour exchange,' she replied. 'Now I'm sixteen I must register with the Ministry of Labour.'

I remembered about all sixteen-years-old girls having to do that so the government will know when it's time for them to be called up for war work.

'You needn't do that,' I said. 'The government would be pretty stupid if they didn't know you were here, wouldn't they?'

They both laughed.

'Margaret,' said Crawfie, 'you'll never need to do war work. You do more than enough by keeping everyone cheerful.'

I suppose that was a compliment, but I hadn't meant to be funny.

# April 26th

Lilibet came back from the labour exchange, and before even bothering to get changed, she telephoned Papa and asked him about doing war work.

When she'd finished speaking, she passed the phone to me, and I had time for a cheery 'hello' and to tell Papa to come back to Windsor for a break from king-work. He said he'd try.

I suspected Lilibet was unhappy, so I went to find her. She was sitting on her bed, and I noticed a new photograph of Philip on her bedside table.

'Are you all right?' I asked.

She smiled, but it wasn't a meaning sort of smile. It looked like it was an effort. 'Yes, Margaret,' she said. 'I'm all right.'

I sat next to her and leaned on her, cuddling her arm. 'Did Papa say no?'

'He said a very definite no,' said Lilibet. 'He says I have my own duty to continue my training and education to be queen.'

'Poor you,' I said. 'It's no fun being a future queen, is it?'

She sighed and unbuckled her Guides belt. 'It isn't meant to be fun, Margaret.'

Then she swung round, gave me a huge hug, and said, 'Thank heaven for sisters! Let's ask for the ponies to be made ready.'

We had a lovely ride – as Lilibet said, to blow the cobwebs out of our hair.

## May 3rd

We cycled slowly round the park this morning, looking at all the places where there used to be flower beds, and now there are vegetables. We even have American officers camped in the park. Mummy's keen to welcome them, and she invites some of the officers to lunch occasionally, which is the most enormous fun. I've learned to speak with an American accent, which drives Mummy and Papa mad! This morning I came to breakfast and said to Lilibet, 'Hi, honey! What's cooking? '

She nearly choked on toast crumbs, which made her eyes water. Lilibet definitely hasn't forgotten about wanting to do her bit. She's still going on about doing nursing in the East End.

'I'd be perfectly safe,' she said. 'No one would know it was me. Who looks in nurses' faces, for goodness sake?'

'Probably everybody does when they're ill,' I said. 'After all, she's the person who's going to make you better or stop you hurting.'

'I suppose so,' said Lilibet.

'Another thing,' I added. 'Papa would never let you sleep in a hotel or a hospital, or wherever nurses sleep. You'd have to come home each night, and that would mean a car taking you. Our cars are bigger than most people's. Don't you think they'd notice?'

She patted my cheek. 'There's something wrong with you, Margaret. You're not yourself.'

'Why?'

'You're actually talking sense!'

'You… you…' I began, but she was already up and running. It was lovely to hear her laugh.


## Later


While I struggled with the wretched sock I'm knitting (pity the poor soldier who gets these), Lilibet sat at a table in the window, reading *Pride and Prejudice*.

'I forgot to tell you,' she said. 'I'm going to be patron of a hospital, so even if I can't do real nursing, maybe I can help raise funds for them.' She gazed out of the window. 'It's not the same, though.'

Just then Crawfie came in. Dookie ran, jumped up at her and scratched her leg with his claws.

'Ow! Dookie, down! That hurt!' said Crawfie.

Lilibet didn't even look round. Some nurse!

## July 5th

We have a lovely new cousin. At least, I'm sure he is lovely, but we haven't seen him yet. He's Prince Michael of Kent. He was born at Coppins, and is Uncle George and Aunt Marina's new baby. So now they have Edward, Alexandra and little Michael.

## July 26th

Sweets are being rationed from today. It doesn't really bother us, as we don't often have them, but Lilibet said how sad it is for evacuees and poor children, who don't have much to keep them cheerful during the war. I must say, though, that when we drive through the streets, I often see children playing, and they look as if they're having fun.

## August 5th

In a week I'll be twelve years old. The war's been going on for almost a quarter of my lifetime.

Everything's changed so much, I can hardly remember what some things were like. Even the view from the castle is different. Papa said it can't have changed a huge amount over the years until now. All that lovely grassland, that made you want to urge your pony into a gallop, is planted with crops. It's like living on a farm.

## August 26th

I want to go back to bed and start the day all over again, and for Lilibet to stay in her bed and not come in to me. I hate the war!

When she did come to my room, Alla and Ruby went out. I could tell from Lilibet's face that something bad had happened. And it has.

Our lovely uncle George has been killed.

I cried and cried, and Lilibet did, too, even though I could tell she was trying to be brave. We cried about Uncle George, and we cried for Papa, who loved his brother.

'What happened?' I asked, when I'd calmed down.

'He was travelling to Iceland in a flying boat, and it crashed,' said Lilibet.

That sent me into fresh floods of tears. Lilibet hugged me the whole time. With Mummy and Papa not being here, I'm so glad of my sister. She's strong and kind.

'Thirteen other people died, Margaret,' said Lilibet. 'We must keep them in our thoughts, too.'

'I will,' I said. 'I'll say a prayer for them, and their families. They must be feeling terrible.'

'It's extra bad for them,' said Lilibet. 'They probably depend on their men for everything.' She stood up. 'Alla will come and sit with you. I'm going to write to Aunt Marina.'

It was then that something seemed to punch me in the middle. 'The little baby,' I cried. 'Little Michael! And poor Alexandra and Edward. They have no father now.'

Suddenly, I forgot my own misery, and thought only of them. I decided to write to the children. But try as I might, the right words wouldn't come. I kept seeing Papa's face before my eyes, and imagining if something bad happened to him. I couldn't bear it. I threw myself on my bed and cried myself to sleep. Alla stroked my hair.

## October 20th

I haven't written my diary for ages. I've written the one Mummy gave us, of course, but it's been full of nothing much. Lilibet has official engagements now, and often goes without me. I don't mind. I get tired of shaking hands and keeping a smile on my face, and trying to remember people's names.

I don't feel well today. Mummy and Papa both have dreadful colds, and I think I'm getting one, too. If I'm not well, perhaps I can have a fire in my bedroom.

How long will it be before we can move back to London, and go to parties and have days at the zoo and all the things we used to do?

## October 28th

Lilibet gets letters from Philip regularly now, but she usually keeps them to herself. Today, though, she told us he's been made first lieutenant on his ship. That means he's the second-in-command, and he's one of the youngest second-in-commands in the navy.

'That's good, isn't it, Papa?' she asked.

'Very good,' he said, smiling. 'But not surprising. Philip has lots of energy, and he's bright. He'll go far, mark my words.'

Lilibet's happy because Philip's doing convoy work, going up and down the east coast of Britain. We're not supposed to know what ships are doing, but she seems to find out.

## November 24th

I'm absolutely worn out. Mummy and Papa gave a Thanksgiving party yesterday in Buckingham Palace. There were a couple of hundred American army and navy officers, and a few nurses. We had some American food: pumpkin pie and sweet potatoes. I liked the sweet potatoes, but I'm not sure about pumpkin pie.

The palace is rather chilly. There doesn't seem to be much heating – that's Papa's effort to economize. In the past, we weren't allowed to wander about the palace on our own, but now Lilibet is older, no one stops us, so we had a prowl round this morning. We were shocked to see parts of it looking so shabby. It must have been pretty badly damaged in the bombing, as I'm sure everyone's worked hard to patch it up and hide the worst of it. Mummy's bedroom windows are still boarded up.

## December 4th

Rehearsals are well under way for our pantomime. This year it's *Sleeping Beauty*, and I am Beauty! Lilibet is my handsome prince, of course, and there's a lot of giggling when she has to 'kiss me up', as one of the evacuees calls it. That's the bit where she kisses me to wake me from my hundred-year sleep.

I can't help thinking what a horrid Christmas it will be for Aunt Marina and our cousins.

# January 7th 1943

Lilibet's on again about doing her bit.

'Papa doesn't want me to be a nurse,' she said when I went into her bedroom to borrow a book about Guides, 'so I must think of something else to do, that he can't say no to.'

'Lilibet, he can say no to anything,' I told her. 'He's our father.'

'But surely he can understand,' she said. 'He and Mummy do their bit, in their way. Oh, I know,' she said, holding up a hand to stop me interrupting, 'we do our knitting and salvaging, but it's not the same and you know it.'

Snappy.

I settled myself at her dressing table and fiddled with her pots and jars. 'Let's see, you could always be a bus conductress. It can't be hard riding around all day selling tickets.' I pretended to think. 'Or you could be a Land Girl, and dig turnips, or get the harvest in while you milk the cows. Or–'

She flounced out of the room, saying, 'Don't be so childish!'

I think somebody hasn't had a letter from Philip lately!

He's due to go to the Mediterranean, and he's said that on his next leave, he's staying with the Mountbattens. She'll like that, because she's bound to see him then. Uncle Dickie always brings him over if he can.

I've received a large sum of money – £20,000 – from one of Granny's friends. She left lots of jewels to Mummy. I'm to buy savings certificates with some of the money, and will put the rest in the bank. It would have been nice to spend some of it, but everyone says, 'Be sensible,' and that Mrs Greville wouldn't want it wasted. I'm sure she wouldn't mind if I bought myself a little treat. What would I buy? Sweets? Rationed. Clothes? Rationed. Oh, I know! I'd take the whole family on a train to the seaside, and we'd build sandcastles and paddle and swim and eat ice creams and that pink stuff – candy floss! Imagine, a whole day of nothing but fun, and no one taking our photographs and no hand-shaking or waving! We'd just be ourselves, like an ordinary family.

## January 22nd

Such a terrible thing happened yesterday. A single German bomber swooped out of the sky and bombed a school south of London. I hope no one was hurt. When I hear about things like that, I feel as if someone's squeezing my heart.

It set Lilibet off again. 'It means children in that area have no school any more. Oh, there's so much work to do,' she said. 'I could help. Other girls my age are doing their bit. Why can't I?'

I could tell her why. She's too important. I wonder if they'd let me do war work, if I was sixteen. The way this war's going, I'll find out in three years. It seems as if it will never end.

## February 27th

Lilibet left Guides yesterday. She's a Sea Ranger now. I want to be one, but Mummy says I've only been in Guides for five minutes.

## March 5th

We looked through some of our photograph albums after lunch. Sometimes it's hard to remember how things looked before the war, when there were no sandbags or air-raid shelters or bombed buildings. Lilibet said, 'London used to look glorious on spring days like today,' and gave a great sigh.

Then we did a little complaining – nowhere near Mummy, of course! – and Lilibet promised everything will be lovely again one day.

We really shouldn't ever grumble. We haven't been bombed out of our home. We don't have to sleep in horrid underground tunnels. We have good food to eat and we don't have to queue for bread.

## April 22nd

Lilibet was seventeen yesterday, and I'll soon be thirteen. Mummy says it's sad that, because of the war, Lilibet can't do half the things she'd normally be doing at her age. We have lots of guests to lunch and to dances and parties, but it's not the same as when the war wasn't on.

But she's going to Coppins while Philip stays there, Aunt Marina said. That made Lilibet's eyes sparkle.

## May 5th

Lilibet was made President of the Royal College of Music a couple of days ago. I actually think I'm a better musician than her. She needs the music in front of her all the time. I don't. If I hear a tune once, I can play it. Or, at least, a pretty good version of it. Still, I suppose they'd rather have the heir to the throne as president than the number two princess.

## May 12th

Women of eighteen must do war work now, by law, even if it's just part-time. Lilibet looked very satisfied when she heard that!

'Papa will have to let me do war work when I'm eighteen,' she said and she walked off singing. But later, I found her writing letters, looking very fed up.

'What's wrong?' I asked. 'You looked so happy this morning, and you've had a letter from Philip.' (There was one on her desk and she was obviously writing back.)

She put the lid on her fountain pen, laid it down, and fondled Dookie's ears. Four dogs were curled up by her feet.

'Mummy and I talked about this war work thing,' she said. 'She explained what I suppose I already knew – that when I'm eighteen I'll be taking on a lot more official duties. I won't be able to do regular work.'

I laughed. 'Just imagine a factory manager, if one of his workers asked for a day off to open a new hospital!' I launched into my impression of what I imagined he'd do, hands behind my back, striding up and down crossly.

'What, Miss Windsor?' I said in a gruff voice. 'What's that you say? Time off to open an 'orspital? Blimey, I'd like time off to open a book, I would, and no mistake!'

Lilibet burst out laughing. 'Make fun of me all you like, but I won't give up nagging Papa!'

## May 20th

We're in London tonight. We went to a service at St Paul's Cathedral today, to thank God for our victory over a German general called Rommel, in North Africa.

As we drew up at the cathedral, Lilibet gasped. (None

of the people watching knew she gasped – she managed to keep her smile and went on waving.)

'What?' I asked.

'Look at the state of the cathedral,' she said.

Great chunks of stone were missing and it looked as if someone had dug bits out of the walls.

'Bomb damage,' she said. 'But at least it's still standing.'

Papa wore his admiral's uniform, and Mummy looked beautiful. As we went in, the people watching made lots of ooh and aah noises. We've hardly ever been in the papers, and I think they're surprised at how much we've grown. My sister looks like a young woman. That makes me feel a bit left behind.


## June 4th


Last night we went to the Strand Theatre, and saw a comedy play called *Arsenic and Old Lace*. It was our very first evening visit to a West End theatre. Mummy said, 'You should have seen the West End before the war. So full of life, and lights and excitement everywhere.'

Well, I thought last night was pretty exciting. Two sweet little girls presented us with posies of flowers, Lilibet first, of course, then me. They curtsied so beautifully, I bet they have ballet lessons.

When we entered our box, the audience, who'd been waiting, stood and cheered! That was a surprise! Afterwards, we went backstage to meet the cast and the backstage workers. There are more people behind the scenes than there are in the play. And it's not nearly as glamorous backstage as it is onstage. I told everyone how much I liked the play, and they seemed pleased.

How wonderful it must be to walk on to the stage of a theatre like the Strand, and see an audience before you. It makes our productions in the Waterloo Chamber seem a little tame. But they're fun.

## July 3rd

Papa's going abroad. I don't know where (I bet Lilibet knows) but I overheard him telling Mummy he won't enjoy the heat, so it must be somewhere hot like Africa.

## July 18th

Mummy's so looking forward to a break at Balmoral. She travels all over the country visiting hospitals and factories and so on. She believes it's important that the people who work quietly in the background are made to realize how much the country values their contribution to the war effort.

I saw some factory workers in a film once. I don't know about working quietly in the background. They kept shrieking to each other, and were obviously having fun, though how they do that and concentrate on what they're making, I don't know!

## July 30th

There, I was right, it was Africa. After our victory, Papa went on a tour of the whole war front in North Africa. Not only that, but he nearly gave everyone, especially Mummy, heart attacks by disappearing for a while. Not disappearing exactly, but he did go missing. He's safely home now, though, and we'll soon be off to Scotland. I hope cousin Margaret's joining us again. She'll be company when Lilibet's on official duties, and even though she's older than me, she treats me just like she treats my sister.

I'm already nagging Crawfie about this year's pantomime. I want us to do *Aladdin*. I've made loads of plans already. She says the schoolmaster, Mr Tanner, needs to have a say in what we do, because he'll be producing it.

'Tell him Princess Margaret would like to do *Aladdin*,' I said. 'Please, Crawfie.'

'Time enough after the summer,' she said. 'Lilibet, would you like to be in the pantomime again this year?'

'Of course!' was the reply. 'But I'd like a different part this year. I always seem to be the prince, and I'm not sure that suits me any more.'

Hmm, she doesn't want to be a prince, but I bet she'd like to be with a prince! I didn't say that, of course. She gets touchy if I tease her about Philip. Personally I think that's because she's a lot more keen on him than he is on her. I talked to Mummy about it the other day, and she said I'm being silly.

'Lilibet and Philip are cousins and just good friends,' she said. 'What's more natural in wartime than that they should write to each other?'

I don't think it's natural that Lilibet should get moody when she doesn't get a letter for ages, or all bright and chipper when she does, or that she should go pink when I tease her.

## August 14th

In a week I'll be in my teen years. I hope everyone will start thinking of me as a young lady instead of a child. I know some people think I look for attention all the time. I don't, not really. Lilibet sticks up for me. She says I'm naturally amusing, so people are happy to listen to me. That makes it sound as if I never stop talking!

## September 11th

It's lovely to be back in Scotland. Lots of people have been to stay and it's turned out to be a summer of hiking, picnics, riding, games in the evenings, dances, a visit to the Highland Games – just so much fun. We've hardly had a moment to call our own. I know Lilibet would have loved Philip to have been one of the visitors. She's brought his photograph with her.

## October 15th

Lilibet was very upset to hear that the husband of one of Philip's sisters has been shot down and killed. I'd normally be sad, too, but the man was a Luftwaffe pilot, and he was in the Nazi SS. I wonder how many of our people he's shot down. Still, I'm sure Philip will be sorry for his sister.

## November 23rd

We've had a lo-o-ong session with Mr Cecil Beaton, the photographer, and his assistants. Oh, they do get on my nerves. I try to keep smiling, but they will fiddle-faddle about so. I have a camera and I take good photographs, but I don't need special lights and little helpers scurrying about. Mummy keeps smiling whatever happens, even if she's ever so slightly seething inside. The pictures will be lovely, though. They always are.

## November 30th

Our air force has bombed Berlin to smithereens. They hit important government buildings, like the ones that control their navy and air force. It's good news, but all Lilibet and I can think about is the people living in the bombed areas – the ordinary German families. They probably don't want the war any more than the ordinary British people do. Yet they're the ones who are killed or injured, or who lose people they love. It's all so cruel.

## December 3rd

We rehearsed for a while today. I got the giggles really badly at one point. It's so funny to see my ladylike sister bounding around the stage. She has such a good time doing these pantomimes.

She's going to have an even better time! Mummy and Papa have invited Philip to visit us over Christmas whenever he can, and they've invited him to see his two cousins on stage. He said yes!

'I'll ask him if he'd like to be in the pantomime with us,' said Lilibet.

I hope he does. That would be really jolly! But whether he does or not, the fact that he's coming has brightened my sister up. Unfortunately, she's now so anxious for her performance to be perfect that she keeps asking me to hear her lines – over and over. I've told her it's not much good just learning the words, you have to practise saying them as you act. I don't know if that's true, but it means we act out all her scenes, with me playing all the other parts. That way I get some fun out of it!

She's often busy these days with learning-to-be-queen stuff, so it's lovely to spend some 'silly' time together.

## December 5th

We tried on our costumes today. One of my Princess Roxana costumes is a gorgeous robe of blue and silver. I tried doing our tap dance in it, and it needs to be shortened if they don't want me falling over the widow's washing basket. That basket will hide Lilibet at the beginning. If she doesn't fall asleep waiting for her cue, she'll burst out of it and surprise the audience. Especially a certain young man who will be sitting in the front row with Mummy and Papa.

This year our cousins Edward and Alexandra will be in our pantomime. Alexandra will be seven on Christmas Day. Michael's too little, but I'm sure he can watch if he's quiet.

## December 19th

The last performance of *Aladdin* was last night. I could hardly drag myself out of bed this morning. Today seems dull. Lilibet's still sparkling, though, because Philip watched one of the performances. Although he flatly refused to be in the show, he was a terrific spectator. He laughed in all the right places, and he clapped madly, especially when we did anything!

Mr Churchill is ill. He's abroad somewhere – we're not being told where. I do hope he gets home soon and has a nice rest over Christmas.

## December 28th

The air force bombed Berlin on Christmas night. How perfectly ghastly. Couldn't they all have stopped the war just for a couple of days?

Our own Christmas was lovely, but that made me feel a little guilty, because so many people are having sad times. I told Philip I was sorry to hear of his brother-in-law's death, and he said a very gruff, 'Thank you very much, Margaret,' and dragged me off to show me a card trick. He likes to keep his feelings to himself, I think. You can usually tell his mood by his eyes. They're very blue, and when he's happy they're just as authors like Enid Blyton describe them – they really do twinkle!

# January 11th 1944

There's no question about it. My sister's in love! When Philip's around, she can't take her eyes off him. When he's not around, she can't stop talking about him. Everyone says that's a sign of love. And if I tease her, she gets cross and pink, then a huge smile spreads across her face and she can't get rid of it!

I love teasing her. But I get more out of her if I don't tease. I asked yesterday if she thought she might marry Philip one day. 'Goodness, Margaret,' she said. 'I'm too young to be thinking about marriage.'

I don't think that's true.

# February 8th

I dropped my scarf when I was out playing with the dogs, so I went to look for it. Two of the gardeners were cutting dead bits off bushes, and I heard one say, 'Something big's on the way, you mark my words.'

The other one said, 'Hitler better watch himself, then.'

'He had, and no mistake,' said the other. 'Mr Churchill's got plans for him, and it ain't inviting him to tea.'

Ooh, that gave me such a thrill. I'll ask Papa if there is 'something big' happening.

## Later

Papa telephoned after lunch, and asked to speak to us. After Lilibet, I took the phone and asked, 'Papa, has Mr Churchill got a secret plan to beat Hitler?'

He was quiet for a moment, then said, 'Why do you ask, Margaret?'

I told him about the gardeners, and he laughed. 'Mr Churchill's fighting fit after his illness, and he's full of plans to beat Hitler, darling. One after the other! Don't worry – we'll win this war. How are your lessons going?'

If Papa's sure we'll win, then I'm sure, too.

# February 29th

Lilibet found me hunched up in my bath robe, reading *Black Beauty* in front of the measly electric fire. We never have coal fires now. We mustn't waste water, or coal or anything else for that matter. Certainly not food.

She closed my book and said, 'Margaret, I've something to tell you.'

'What?'

Lilibet put her arm round me and said, 'It's sad news. Our cousin George – George Lascelles – has been wounded.'

I put my hand to my mouth.

'He's all right, though,' she went on. 'But the poor young man has been put in a horrid prison called Colditz Castle.'

'Colditz,' I repeated. 'What a horrible name. Poor George.'

'But listen! Papa said that even though the Germans insist that Colditz is escape-proof, officers have escaped from there. In fact, two of them simply walked out!'

'Don't be silly,' I said. 'There must be guards.'

'It's true! They wore fake German uniforms, made

by the prisoners, and had false papers. One of them, Mr Churchill told Papa, even had the colossal cheek to order a soldier to salute!'

I laughed, then I got upset again about George, but Lilibet grabbed my hands.

'Margaret, don't you see? If they can escape, maybe George can.'

How exciting to think that our own cousin might escape the Nazis. Exciting, but scary.

Lilibet hugged me. 'Let's hope this beastly war's soon over, then all the chaps who've been imprisoned can come home to their families. Aunt Mary must be feeling dreadful about George. Thank goodness she has war duties to occupy her.'

'War duties?'

'Yes, she's Commandant of the ATS.' Lilibet saw my blank look and explained, 'Auxiliary Territorial Service – it's the women's branch of the army. She travels all over, visiting ATS units.' She put my book back in my lap and stood up. 'I must write to her. Perhaps I can visit her. I'll ask Mummy.'

My sister will be a wonderful queen. She doesn't always show it, but inside she really cares about everybody.

## March 16th

Lilibet practically wrenched my arm off this morning as I was putting my hat on. She flew into the hall, grabbed me and dragged me outside. 'Margaret, you'll never guess!'

Of course, I did guess immediately, that Philip's coming to visit, so I decided to tease her. 'Give me three goes,' I said.

She waited impatiently as I pretended to think.

'Don't scowl,' I said. 'You'll get wrinkles on your forehead, and they'll look terrible when your portrait's on pound notes.'

'Ooh, you –'

I dodged out of her grasp and said, 'All right, sourpuss, I'm guessing. Let's see … umm … You've got a new fountain pen?' (Lilibet is very fussy about her pens.)

'No.'

'One of the dogs is having puppies?'

'No!'

'Right. Last go. Could it be … Philip's coming to stay?'

'No!'

'No?' That took me by surprise. 'What, then?'

She pulled me beneath the branches of a cedar tree. 'Promise not to say anything to anyone?'

This sounded good! 'Cross my heart and hope to die.'

'King George of Greece has asked Papa to support Philip's application to become a British citizen!'

'Oh. Isn't he one already?'

'No, silly. Prince Philip of Greece and Denmark?'

I couldn't see why it was so important, until suddenly daylight dawned. Perhaps Philip wants to become British so he can marry Lilibet. Is that what she was thinking? But he couldn't have asked her to marry him, first because he'd have to ask Papa's permission, and second, if he had, her face would be lit up like the sun. Anyway, she's only seventeen.

I felt confused. If I said he might want to marry her, and he didn't, I would never forgive myself, because she'd be mortified. But surely that's what she's thinking?

Luckily, a footman hobbled over to ask us to go to the Queen's drawing room. Lilibet asked why he was limping.

'I fell over a corgi, Ma'am.'

'Oh dear, they do fall asleep in odd places, don't they?' she said. He looked uncomfortable. 'Is that what happened?' she asked.

'No, Ma'am,' said the footman. 'He was trying to bite me.'

I coughed to smother my giggles. Lilibet simply twitched.

## Later

If Philip has let Lilibet think he might want to marry her, he'd better not let her down, that's all I can say. I would never, ever forgive him. I want him to love her as much as we all do.

## April 3rd

Great plans are afoot, Lilibet told me, as she pulled out our big map of Europe. We're going to invade Germany. It's one of those things everyone seems to know about, but no one's saying anything. Papa knows, of course, so I'm sure Mummy does, too. That must be how Lilibet knows. Her eighteenth birthday's coming up. It's a very important one for her, as heir to the throne.

## April 24th

My sister is grown-up. It's official. She's now eighteen and is a Counsellor of State. That means she can sign things on behalf of the King, if he's away, for instance, along with the three other Counsellors. They are Uncle Henry, the Duke of Gloucester, Aunt Mary, the Princess Royal, and cousin Alexandra, Princess Arthur of Connaught. It's a terribly responsible thing.

She had the most gorgeous mink coat, and two more pearls from Papa. She has thirty-six now – three more years and she'll have the full set.

Mummy and Papa gave her a horse, and she has her own new little corgi pup, called Susan. That's a sweet name. I told Lilibet that if I ever have a baby daughter, I shall call her Susan.

'Would you seriously name a princess after a dog?'

'Granny had a dog called Elizabeth when you were born,' I said.

She looked appalled. 'No!' Then she burst out laughing, and threw a dog biscuit at me.

The Grenadier Guards were on parade for Lilibet's

birthday; this time they presented her with their Colour. It's a flag that's very special to them, made of deep red silk, with Lilibet's initial embroidered on it, and a coronet above.

Thank goodness, she had a card from Philip. He's staying in the north of England while his ship's being prepared for sea.

We also had a lovely outing to see a musical comedy called *Something in the Air* at the Palace Theatre in Shaftesbury Avenue. It was very jolly. I sang a song called 'Yom Pom Pom' all the way back to the palace. It's not that far, so I don't know why everyone was groaning by the time we arrived. They should be pleased to have free entertainment. 'Yom pom pom, chirra chirra bim bom!'

## May 15th

The invasion's soon. It must be. Every time we go out in the car, we see hordes of soldiers and army vehicles heading south. Papa said that coming from London the other night, he passed a field full of army tents. Next morning, he went back after breakfast and the field was empty!

'You imagined it,' Lilibet said.

'Indeed I did not,' he said crossly, but then he saw her mouth twitching, and he laughed.

We can guess where the soldiers have gone. To the south coast!

Oh, please, please let this be the end of the war. I so long to be back in London all the time, going to dances and parties and theatres and the ballet.

## June 10th

When it did come, there was no mistaking it. D-Day! From early morning, the sky was filled with aeroplanes, all growling off in the same direction. Papa and Mummy were in London, so we had to wait to find out what was happening.

During the night and early morning, men landed on the beaches of Normandy, in France. They fought their way ashore. Canada and America were part of the invasion. They broke through the German defences, and are on their way to victory!

# June 14th

I don't like it. Papa's going to visit the men on the Normandy beaches.

'I'm sure Mr Churchill wouldn't let him go if it was dangerous,' said Lilibet. 'We can't do anything about it, Margaret, so we must just keep calm and carry on.'

I laughed. 'You sound like one of those men on the wireless who say things like, "Remember, careless talk costs lives!"'

She smiled. 'Come on, let's tackle some piano duets. We haven't played together for ages.'

'No, it's too nice out,' I said. 'Let's go for a walk and talk about what it'll be like when the war's over.'

I love doing that.

# June 19th

Just as I thought we were winning the war and the Nazis would leave us alone, something ghastly's happening. They're sending flying bombs over. They're like aeroplanes, but without pilots. When they get over their target, the engine stops and the bomb plummets to earth and explodes.

Yesterday one landed on the Guards Chapel near Buckingham Palace. Over a hundred people were killed, and a hundred more injured. The flying bombs are nicknamed doodlebugs, and they're coming over in droves.

Crawfie said a doodlebug landed on Windsor a few days ago. It started a fire, and two people were killed. That's too close.

# 28th June

One of those beastly doodlebugs has destroyed the palace tennis court. I'm glad no one was playing tennis at the time.

Hundreds upon hundreds of people have been killed by these hateful rocket things, and thousands injured. The trouble is that on a cloudy day you can't see the doodlebug. When the engine cuts out, there's complete silence, and suddenly the thing nose dives to the ground and – boom! No time to get out of the way.

Mummy says Londoners are beginning to evacuate again.

I burst into tears after hearing about our tennis court. I suppose it was a shock, because Papa loved to play tennis there. Lilibet cuddled me. 'I know,' she said, 'I know.'

'But it was all going to be all right,' I sobbed. 'Mr Churchill had plans, and we invaded France and beat the Germans there, and they're not beaten at all.'

'You should listen more carefully when Papa's talking,' she said. 'Britain has rallied round and we have marvellous defences against the doodlebugs.'

I sniffed. 'Have we?'

'We certainly have,' she said, fishing out her handkerchief. 'Here, dry your eyes.'

'What defences?' I asked. I suspected she was making it up to make me feel better, but I should have known she wouldn't do that. She's too honest.

'Fighter planes,' she said. 'Hundreds of them over the Channel. They try to shoot the doodlebugs down, but any that get through run into a barrage of balloons just inland – that brings them down. If any slip through, we've more fighters waiting for them. You'll see,' she finished with a smile.

I blew my nose. 'That's good.'

'Have you practised your speech yet?'

My stomach turned over. 'I'll fetch it now, and you can listen to it.' I held out her handkerchief. 'Thanks.'

She put both hands up, palms out. 'You can keep it.'


## July 3rd


The day's nearly here for Mummy and me to visit a school in Windsor. I'm to make a speech in the afternoon. I've practised so many times, I know it off by heart, but I feel sick every time I think of doing it. Papa has difficulty with speeches, I know, but Mummy doesn't, and Lilibet was just amazing when she made her first speech. It was as if she'd done it a hundred times before.

But I haven't done it a hundred times, and I'm nervous. I'd almost rather sing the children a song.

No, I wouldn't.

## July 5th

Too many doodlebugs have landed on Windsor for my liking.
I wonder if they're aimed at the castle.

## July 23rd

Lilibet and I are in London tonight, and it's strangely quiet.
Thousands of people have evacuated because of doodlebugs.
We heard one flying overhead when we were walking in the
park at Windsor today. You've never seen anyone move so
fast. Lilibet grabbed my hand and we raced, bent over, to
the nearest trench, and leaped into it. Good thing I've been
practising running-to-safety-in-the-trenches at Guides!
Luckily, the doodlebug continued on its way. Luckily for us,
but not for the poor souls where it finally landed.

Papa left today for a tour of the troops. We're not allowed
to know exactly where he's going. No one is except the
prime minister and Papa's own people, and the top army

133

officers. None of the staff even know he's gone away, and we're not telling. We can't put Papa's life in danger by leaking information to the wrong people.

Lilibet's now in her role as Counsellor of State and will act for Papa, signing things and so on, in the Privy Council. They're Papa's top advisers. She also has to go on visits, not just to military people, but to ordinary ones, too. I suppose I'll do that sort of thing in a couple of years' time. I hope I can do it as calmly and carefully as Lilibet. I hope I can trust myself to get it right!

I did make a jolly good job of my speech at that school, though I say so myself. My skirt hid my shaky knees! Mummy said she was proud of me, and it was comforting to have her sitting smiling up at me. Papa always says she's a soothing presence when he does something difficult. He means speeches.

Lilibet has made two visits to Aunt Marina at Coppins, and each time Philip was there! I wonder...

He's left to join his ship now, so she's sad, but she'll have nice memories. And there'll be lots of letters, I'm sure.

## August 25th

Great news! Our armed forces have freed Paris from the Nazis! Imagine how happy the French people must be. Papa said, 'Wine will flow freely tonight!'

Not many doodlebugs get through these days. Oh, it's wonderful! Things are turning in our favour. I wish that fiend (as Granny calls him) Hitler would just give up. He must know he's going to be beaten.

## September 9th

Good news and bad news.

The good news is that Belgium has been liberated from the Nazis. They're free.

The bad news is that, far from giving up, Hitler's fighting back with a terrible new weapon. I must keep it a deathly secret, because Mr Churchill doesn't want the people to know about it, in case it starts panic.

It's a new type of doodlebug. The first one was officially known as the V1. This is the V2, and it's even more powerful. It flies faster than the speed of sound, and no one knows it's coming. The explosion makes a huge crater in the ground, and everything around it is destroyed. The people are being told that the explosions are from gas mains, whatever they are. All I know is my papa looks terribly strained.

An awful thought has hit me. If the king shares the responsibility for his people with the prime minister, leading the country through war could be something my lovely, pretty sister will have to do one day. Well, I'll be there for her. She can share it with me, too. Alla always says, 'A trouble shared is a trouble halved.'

But I'll always be thankful that it's not me who'll be queen.

## September 20th

Mummy said there haven't been any of those horrid V2 rockets for a couple of days now. Perhaps the Nazis have run out.

I've knitted my first sock without dropping stitches and having to have them rescued. Lilibet said we should tell the newspapers, so I hit her on the head with *The Times*!

## October 5th

I spoke too soon. The V2s are back. I don't know if Londoners really believe the explosions are all caused by gas.

Papa's going abroad again soon, to visit troops in Holland. Strange to think that not so long ago he wouldn't have been able to do that, because the country was overrun by Germans.

## October 26th

Princess Beatrice has died. She was eighty-seven, which is an enormous age. Her mother was Queen Victoria, whose reign, apart from one year, was in the last century. From where I'm sitting, I can see her portrait. How old-fashioned she seems to us twentieth century girls.

## November 4th

Lilibet talked today about our grandfather – Mummy's father, the Earl of Strathmore.

'He's not well at all,' she said.

'Is it his chest again?' I asked. He had the most dreadful cough last time we saw him.

She nodded. 'He has bronchitis. It's very bad, Margaret.'

The way she said it made me stop asking questions, because I didn't want to hear the answers.

Poor Mummy must be terribly worried.

## November 8th

Our grandfather died yesterday. He was such a sweetie – deaf as a post, but he always smiled as if he could hear what I was saying. Uncle Patrick will be the Earl now, as he's the oldest son.

Poor Mummy. She's so brave.

## November 27th

A beastly, horrible thing happened on Saturday. A V2 rocket hit a Woolworths shop in London. It was lunchtime, so lots of workers were in there shopping. Nearly 150 people were killed, but more may have died since. Of course, the people know now that these massive explosions aren't caused by gas. The prime minister told them a couple of weeks ago. How terrifying to know you could be wiped out in an instant, all because that mad Hitler wants to take over the world.

Our pantomime's well under way now. It's going to be different this year. It's called *Old Mother Red Riding Boots*. And for once, Lilibet will play a lady!

## December 5th

Lilibet was upset this morning, because Philip's father, Prince Andrew of Greece, died in Monaco on Sunday.

'I know Philip hasn't seen him for years,' she said, 'and, to be honest, I don't believe they were close. But still, it's terrible to lose your father. Look how awful it's been for Mummy. He was only sixty-two.'

'Poor man,' I said, 'but that's quite old, isn't it?'

'Not at all,' she said. 'Papa's nearly fifty.'

Fifty seems old to me, but my papa's not old.

'Does Philip know?' I asked.

'I believe his grandmother told him. He's in Ceylon at the moment.'

'You shouldn't tell me that,' I said teasingly. 'Walls have ears, you know!'

She looked at me severely. 'Margaret, there's a time and a place for humour.'

Ooh. She is grown-up.

I'm sorry for Philip, though. His family's spread about all over the place. I don't know how any of them can be close. I'm so thankful for my little family. Even when they get cross with me!

## January 24th 1945

Papa has at last given in to Lilibet's pleas to be allowed to do her bit for the war effort. She's going to join the ATS.

An officer called Junior Commander Violet Wellesley is teaching her to drive a car, and then she's going on a course at Camberley, to learn to drive big vehicles like trucks and ambulances, and to look after them. She'll be 230873 2nd Subaltern Elizabeth Windsor of the Auxiliary Territorial Service. She's been measured for her uniform and Papa says she's bouncing with excitement. He's so sweet – I know he'd rather she stayed at home and just did official duties. But she's so determined.

## February 4th

We're spending far more time at Buckingham Palace now. It's good, because we see old friends, and have lots of visitors and parties. Everything's much livelier.

Lilibet has plenty of official engagements planned – all sorts of things. She'll be opening schools, visiting hospitals, taking salutes and so on. Sometimes she represents Papa. For instance, she went to officially wave off Uncle Henry, the Duke of Gloucester, when he went to Australia to become their governor-general. Papa couldn't go, so she stood in for him.

Because she's so busy, there are loads of travel discussions, dress fittings, and lots and lots of hats. Some of the clothes and hats might appear new, but they're often old ones made over with different trimmings to give them a fresh look. Lilibet laughed when I joined her for an outfit-selection session.

'Are you honestly interested in the clothes I'm wearing to an exhibition?' she asked.

'No,' I said, 'I'm waiting for you to grow out of them. Lilibet, you really should eat more!'

She sometimes offers to do engagements for Papa. I know why. It's because he looks so tired these days.

'He has so much to worry about,' she said, as she interfered with the jigsaw I was doing. 'He knows far more about the war than anybody except Mr Churchill. I believe that one day we'll all be told things we never dreamed of. "Dream" is probably the wrong word,' she added. 'I think "nightmare" might be more fitting. There,' she said, pressing rather too hard on a puzzle piece. 'That's the missing bit of the church clock.'

'It's actually a bit of ship's rigging,' I said, trying to prise it out. 'I'll finish this myself, thanks. You go and have tea. I'll be along soon.'

It's nice to have time to myself, because we're always busy these days. I'm not complaining! It's lovely to be invited to some of the parties Lilibet goes to and, of course, when Mummy gives little dances for her at the palace or Windsor, I go, too. I love dressing up and swapping jewels for the evening with Lilibet. She has more than me. And I absolutely adore the music and dancing.

We frequently have guests at Windsor, and Mummy invites lots of young men. The place is often crawling with Guards officers. Lilibet's noticed, too.

'Margaret, every one of our male guests for next Friday is what Mummy and Granny would call "suitable",' she said.

'You mean they're for you to choose a boyfriend?' I asked.

'I think that's the general idea,' she said. 'Oh, I wish Philip was here. Not for any particular reason,' she added hastily. 'But he is rather fun.'

I think Mummy's invited those young men *because* Philip isn't here. Perhaps she hopes Lilibet will take a fancy to one of them.

My sister usually knows her own mind. I've noticed that as she's grown older, she looks at things from all angles before making decisions. And if people don't agree with her, she's liable to dig her heels in.

She wants Philip.

## February 11th

Lilibet has joined the ATS. She can't go every day, of course. One thing Papa's insisted on is that she comes home every evening. But she's determined that when she's on duty, she's to be treated just like the other women. She means it, too.

When the war's over, Lilibet and Philip will both be able to say, 'During the war, when I was a serving officer…'

I won't. Left-at-home Margaret, I'll be.

## March 3rd

Lilibet is definitely in love with Philip. She told me. Well, not in so many words. She's always careful in what she says, but I know her too well. She loves him. I hope he loves her. He'd better.

I did ask Mummy if she thought Philip might propose to Lilibet. She laughed that little light laugh of hers that isn't really a laugh, but gives her time to think.

'Who can foretell the future, darling?' she said.

I waited. I thought that if I kept quiet, Mummy might keep talking. She did.

'We like Philip very much, of course we do,' she said, 'and he's certainly proved himself in the war. He's a fine young man, and I know Lilibet is fond of him. But…'

Again, I waited.

'But she's so young. Too young to know her own feelings.'

'Mummy, she's eighteen. Grown up.'

Mummy had all sorts of 'buts'. But they don't really know each other. But he has no proper home. But he may not be as fond of Lilibet as she is of him. It went on and on.

She ended by saying, 'Lilibet meets lots of eligible young men. Who knows what will happen?'

For once, I think Mummy's wrong, wrong, wrong.


## March 4th


Lilibet's old tutor, Mr Marten, is now Sir Henry Marten. Papa knighted him on the steps of Eton College Chapel today. It was lovely. Lilibet gave him a beautiful smile. She's fond of him.

'He's such a character, and he's been a wonderful teacher,'

she said. 'I thought constitutional history would be dry and dusty, but he made it so interesting.'

Sir Henry must be about seventy, and he looks a dear. The boys gave him three mighty cheers. Lilibet says he's been teaching at Eton for ever. It's nice that he gets a reward for all he's done, especially for packing my sister's head with so much history.

## March 7th

Oh, I cannot wait to grow up. Lilibet has such a good time. She's adoring being in the army. Most mornings she gets collected by car, has a lovely time with 'the girls' and comes home in the evening, bursting with funny stories. The drivers learn how to look after their vehicles, so she talks about spark plugs and axles, changing tyres and goodness knows what else. She also told us she takes her turn serving meals! Yesterday she drove us around the park in Papa's car. It was a bit jerky, but she's really good. We passed some people out walking, and they absolutely gaped to see Princess Elizabeth at the wheel and the King of England holding on for dear life!

She still has to do official engagements, but she's glad to do them, and is always smiling in the photographs. I'm not quite as smiley. Sometimes she nudges me and hisses, 'Smile,' and still edges me towards where I'm supposed to stand. It's a bit bossy, but it does stop me forgetting myself and going wrong.

Lilibet has her own suite in Buckingham Palace now, and a new lady-in-waiting, called Jean. The poor woman lost her husband a few months ago, and she's quite young. She'll have fun with Lilibet and Mary, another lady-in-waiting. They do dreary things like answer letters, but they also go on official engagements, which must be lovely if you haven't got to make a speech!

## March 20th

We went to see 2nd Subaltern Elizabeth Windsor at work today! It was funny seeing her in overalls, with her head under the bonnet. Her tools were spread out on a cloth on the ground, and she carefully told me what they were all called. Yawn.

Mummy had a careful look at the engine, which filthy, and asked what Lilibet was doing. I'm sure she didn't understand a word of the reply.

I feel so proud that my sister's doing what all those other women soldiers do.

## April 13th

I hardly see Lilibet these days. She goes to bed straight after dinner most evenings.

'I've never worked so hard in my life,' she told Alla one evening, as she flopped into an armchair and put her slippered feet on a footstool. Mummy and Papa were out for the evening, so we had supper with Alla in the nursery, like the old days.

'I wish I could join up,' I said. 'Wouldn't it be fun to go together?'

She smiled. I don't suppose she agrees. It's not often a princess can do something on her own without the family and drivers and detectives around. As I know, only too well.

## Later

I've just heard the news that President Roosevelt died yesterday. It's such a shame – he was going to come to

London, but we'll never meet him now. The American people must be very sad.

The new president is the old vice-president, Harry S. Truman. He was sworn in straight away. They don't waste time in the United States.

It's such a shame that President Roosevelt didn't live to see the end of the war. We're sure it can't be far off.

## April 30th

Another victory! In Italy! The German forces there have surrendered, and Hitler's ally, Mussolini, has been captured and shot.

Can the end of the war be far away? Poor Lilibet, she's only just joined up!

## May 1st

~~The most wonderful news!~~ Adolf Hitler is dead!

Oh dear. I wish I was using pencil. I could rub that first

sentence out. It's bad to feel like that about a dead person, even when they've done the most evil things, as Papa says Hitler has.

Does this mean the war's finished?

No, Crawfie's just been in. She says someone will take over as German leader. I hope he's not as bad as Hitler. Lilibet said there have been horrors I wouldn't believe. I don't think I want to know about horrors.

## May 5th

Things move so fast! The German forces in Holland, Denmark and even part of Germany have surrendered!

Papa said he and Mummy should have stayed in London. She said a few days in the country does anyone good, and there's nothing Papa needs to do that can't be done at Windsor. 'If you're needed in town, I'm sure Mr Churchill will let you know,' she said. Matter closed.

## Later

Lilibet just looked in, with a big beaming smile, to say that the German forces in Norway have surrendered. There can't be many left!

## May 6th

What a day!

We were all ready for church, hats on, when a message came for Papa. He and Mummy were needed urgently in London.

We all jumped into the car and headed for the city. Papa was quiet, and looked tired, but his eyes were brighter than they've been for ages.

Uniformed officers and other men are in and out of Buckingham Palace. We know exactly what's going on. In the next few hours, Germany will sign a document officially surrendering.

We've won the war!

Lilibet said quietly, 'How privileged we are to know this before the rest of the world.'

## May 7th

I wanted to stay up last night so I didn't miss anything, but I was packed off to bed and told it would all be the same whether I was asleep or awake.

Lilibet and the dogs brought me the news this morning. Germany officially surrendered at 2.41 a.m.

I danced around the room. 'We won! We won!'

She sat on my bed and let me caper about for a bit, with the dogs darting about my feet, then said, 'Don't forget, Margaret, Japan hasn't surrendered. We're still at war.'

That stopped me. 'Oh.' Then I remembered. 'Philip's out there, isn't he?'

She nodded. 'Somewhere in the Pacific Ocean. I hope he's safe.'

I put my arms round her. 'There was I, all happy, and you're missing Philip so very, very much. Sorry.'

Lilibet kissed my forehead. 'Nothing to be sorry about.' She checked her watch. 'I must fly.'

As she left I thought, Hmm, she's missing Philip 'so very, very much'.

For once, she hadn't said, 'Don't be silly, Margaret.'

## Later

Victory in Europe Day, which everyone's calling VE Day, is tomorrow, and Mr Churchill will officially announce the end of the war in Europe. Lilibet said it'll be a day of celebration like we haven't seen since Papa and Mummy's coronation. How exciting!

## May 8th, VE Day

We woke to freedom! Rain, too, but it didn't last.

At breakfast, Mummy told us Mr Churchill was coming to lunch, then Papa rushed in.

'You must see what's happening in the Mall. Hurry!'

Well, of course, Mummy never hurries. I was first

there, and I twitched the edge of the curtains. 'Look at the crowds!' I cried.

From every direction, men, women and children poured into the Mall. What's more, they were singing as they came. Some linked arms and marched in step. And the colours! It was as if someone had decided to brighten up dreary old London by opening their paintbox and brushing it with red, white, blue and every other colour! Children waved flags, and everyone was happy.

I stayed near the window all morning. The cheering, dancing people never knew a young princess was watching and wishing she could be dancing with them. At one point, cousin Margaret joined us. She's staying here with her brother Andrew, but she goes out to work so I don't see her often.

At lunch, I've never seen two men shake hands as warmly as Papa did with Mr Churchill. We left them talking, and Mummy took us into the garden for some fresh air. As we walked across the lawn, Lilibet looked at me, and I looked at her.

'Race you!' she said, and we were off, with Mummy's 'Darlings!' ringing in our ears and dogs yapping at our heels.

We headed for the hillock where we stood when we were little, trying to glimpse the outside. Now, when we stood there and stretched up, we could see a sea of heads bobbing along beyond the wall.

'Look at those hats!' Lilibet laughed.

There were some silly ones: a perfectly normal bowler hat, with a Union Jack stuck in the top; another with red, white and blue streamers coming out of it like a fountain. Everyone was smiling or singing. It was wonderful to know that no aeroplane would dive out of the clouds with guns blazing.

We ran back to Mummy and strolled with her.

'Now Papa can take it easier, can't he?' I said.

She smiled. 'I hope so, Margaret.'

'But London's problems aren't over,' said Lilibet.

'What do you mean?'

'You've seen it for yourself,' she said. 'Bombed houses mean people with nowhere to live. Bombed railway stations mean people can't get to work. A bombed school means nowhere for children to learn. There's so much to do.'

I squeezed her hand. 'Mr Churchill will sort everything out, won't he?'

'I hope so,' said Lilibet. 'Come on, dogs!' And off she ran. It's nice to see her so relaxed.

Back indoors, we sat by an open window, behind the curtain, watching the crowds in the Mall. Then Mummy called us to listen to the wireless. At three o'clock exactly, the announcer said, 'This is London. The prime minister… the Right Honourable Winston Churchill…'

And Mr Churchill, sitting in his Downing Street office, began his speech. It was long, and complicated, but I remember he said, 'Hostilities will end officially at one minute after midnight tonight,' which sounded odd to me when everyone seems to be having a party already! He said our dear Channel Islands are to be freed today. The Germans actually invaded them and have been living there.

Then he said we can rejoice for a while, but we mustn't forget that we haven't yet beaten Japan. I glanced at Lilibet. She was nibbling her lip, and I know who she was thinking of.

Mr Churchill ended with 'God Save the King!' and we all gave a little cheer. Lilibet and I went back to our window overlooking the Mall.

'I've never seen so many happy people in one place in my life,' I said.

Lilibet said thoughtfully, 'I don't believe they're all completely happy.'

I looked at her as if she was mad. 'What do you mean?'

'Just think,' she said. 'All those bombed houses, stations, factories, schools. So many people lost loved ones in the war. How they must wish they were here to share the joy.'

We spotted horses and riders trying to force a way through the crowds. There were cars behind them. As the people parted to let them through, there were bursts of fresh cheering. People scrambled up lampposts for a better view.

'Who is it, Lilibet?'

'I can't tell,' she said. 'Wait a minute … I know who it is! Here's a clue – big, fat cigar.'

'Mr Churchill!' I said.

Indeed it was.

A message came: 'Please join Their Majesties for a balcony appearance.' As we checked each other's hair, and made our way to the centre room, we could still hear the crowd. They shouted, 'We want the King!'

The room was crowded with family, friends and complete strangers. 'Ready, girls?' said Papa.

'But they're shouting for you,' said Lilibet.

'We come as a package,' said Papa. 'Come on, the four of us.'

The doors were opened, and as we stepped forward, the roar of the crowd was so loud I felt I could almost touch it. We waved and waved, and then suddenly, the whole crowd joined together, singing, 'For He's a Jolly Good Fellow'. I got a lump in my throat.

We made several more balcony appearances. It might have been my imagination, but when Mr Churchill eventually managed to join us, the roar of delight from the crowd was even louder than before. Then they hushed. He stepped forward and bowed to the people. They exploded with more cheers!

He stood between Mummy and Papa (thank goodness he didn't have one of his smelly cigars) and I think he was taken aback by what someone in the room behind called an 'emotional outpouring'.

The whole day was a muddle, with people in and out, and

tea and sandwiches being served at odd times. When evening came, the most wonderful thing happened. Searchlight beams pierced the sky, and for once they weren't looking for enemies. They shone in celebration! Floodlights lit the palace. Mummy had changed into a white dress and tiara, and she sparkled in the lights.

'Fireworks!' Lilibet pointed. 'How long since we've seen fireworks!'

We could barely hear the firework explosions because of the din of the crowd. More and more people joined them.

After our umpteenth balcony appearance, Lilibet had the best brainwave ever.

'Crawfie,' she said, grabbing our passing governess, 'come and stand up for me.' She went to Papa. 'May we go out there?'

He looked at her as if she'd gone mad. 'Out there?'

'Listen to them shouting for you,' she said. 'They love you. They love us. We couldn't possibly come to any harm.'

'We?' I said. 'Me, too?'

Lilibet turned. 'Of course you, too!'

Papa looked at Mummy. Lilibet looked at Papa. I held my breath. Cousin Margaret had heard, too. She gripped Lilibet's arm and waited for the answer.

Papa looked around the room, at Mummy, Crawfie, and finally at Lilibet. 'You may –' he began.

Lilibet, cousin Margaret and I jumped up and down with

excitement, but Papa went on, 'You may, as long as Margaret's brother goes, too. Crawfie, you'll go, won't you?'

She nodded, smiling.

'Take a lady-in-waiting, oh, and a couple of Guards officers…'

In the end, a whole gang of us went out, including Uncle David (Mummy's brother), some uniformed Guards, Papa's equerry, who carried his umbrella everywhere, Margaret, Andrew (her brother), Lilibet and me. We slipped out of a side gate, and we girls linked arms as we walked up the Mall, just following our noses. At one point, I looked at Lilibet in her uniform, and cousin Margaret all grown up, and remembered times before the war, when we played circuses together at Balmoral. The world has changed since then.

But tonight was for fun! We joined in singing 'Roll Out The Barrel', and 'Run, Rabbit, Run'. I know all the words. I remember dancing to 'Knees Up Mother Brown' along Piccadilly, past a burning dummy of Hitler and a little white dog wearing a Union Jack coat! How different London looks all lit up. We joined a conga line and danced into the Ritz Hotel through one door and out again through another. Boats on the Thames hooted and sounded their sirens, but you could barely hear them for the noise of the revellers!

It must have been after midnight before we were standing with the crowd looking up at dear old Buckingham Palace, with all her war wounds lit up by the floodlights.

The balcony, draped in gold-fringed scarlet, looks tiny from down below. The crowd shouted, 'We want the King,' so we joined in!

'We want the King!' I bellowed. At one point I glanced at Lilibet. Her eyes were glistening as she stood quietly amid the racket. I guessed she must be thinking, 'I want my prince.' I squeezed her hand.

She smiled quickly, and a voice nearby said, 'See that girl? She looks like Princess Elizabeth.'

'Time to go, I think,' said Uncle David, his voice hoarse from singing and cheering. We went to a gate and Lilibet said to the policeman on duty, 'May we go in, please?'

His mouth fell open, which made us laugh. And when I walked past him and said, 'Thank you,' it fell open even more!

It was a wonderful, wonderful day.

## May 9th

I'm so tired. We all went out this afternoon, driving through the East End. It's totally devastated. I hope never to see anything like that in our country ever again.

## May 25th

There've been so many celebrations to attend! Lots of victory parades, and today a special thanksgiving service at St Paul's Cathedral. Lilibet and I rode backwards in the carriage, of course – yuk. We had an escort of the Household Cavalry, who all looked wonderful. They must have been polishing their uniforms – and their horses – all night! It's so lovely to have magnificent processions again. Last night there was a celebration concert at the Royal Albert Hall. Tonight I'm so tired, I can hardly move. Victory's exhausting!

## June 6th

Mummy and Papa are off to the Channel Islands for a visit tomorrow. I wish I could go. I've never been abroad. I know the Channel Islands aren't exactly abroad, but you do have to go by ship or aeroplane.

## July 5th

It's general election day. I don't know why they're bothering. How could anyone vote for someone other than Mr Churchill, after all he's done for our country? Anyway, we won't know the results for ages, because in some parts of the country, voting's later in the month. Also, there are lots of votes to come in from people serving in the forces overseas. They must all have their say.

## July 26th

I don't believe it! Lilibet can't believe it! Papa says it's the way of the world. Mr Churchill has lost the election. Our new prime minister is Mr Clement Attlee, the leader of the Labour party.

I don't understand. Mr Churchill's a hero! Well, I hope Mr Attlee does just as good a job of leading the country. He's with Papa right this minute.

## August 2nd

Lilibet said at breakfast, 'President Roosevelt wasn't able to visit us, but at least we can offer a British welcome to President Truman.'

'Is he coming over?' I asked.

'Margaret, Papa's going to meet him today! Where has your head been?

In my wretched school books, that's where my head's been.

I really thought that when the war was over, everything would be different, but it's all just the same. The only difference is that I don't have Lilibet's company in the schoolroom and I hardly see her except when we're doing official things.

Oh well, there'll be a big reception for the president. That will liven things up.

## August 5th

Papa has had talks with President Truman, and so has Mr Attlee. When Papa flops down in Mummy's sitting room afterwards, he looks absolutely exhausted. He never usually wants to talk about anything that was discussed, but Lilibet told me that tonight he sent everyone out of the room, footmen and all, and talked privately to Mummy.

'Everybody has to talk to someone,' she said. 'Even a king.'

When she becomes queen, which I hope will be when she's a lot, lot older, she'll need someone to talk to. I'll be there for her.

But I think she'd prefer that someone to be Philip.

## August 7th

There's been the most terrible thing. Yesterday an American aeroplane dropped a bomb on a place called Hiroshima, in Japan. Papa said almost three quarters of the city was wiped out, flattened. With one bomb! But this was nothing like the bombs in the war. It was far worse – worse than the V2s, even. It's called an atomic bomb and it even had a name: 'Little Boy'. They say it must have killed at least eighty thousand people.

I shall pray that nothing like that ever happens again, anywhere in the world.

## August 10th

The Americans had another bomb. It was called 'Fat Man'. Yesterday they dropped it on a Japanese city, called Nagasaki. Thousands and thousands more people are dead.

Papa looks grey. Lilibet is as agitated as it's possible to

be, because she knows Philip's in Tokyo Bay. I begged her to come and play tennis, to take her mind off him, but he was all she talked about as we changed ends. It was 'Philip wrote that…' and 'When Philip comes back…' all the time. He writes practically every week, so there was plenty to say. In the end, we gave up tennis and sat on a bench and chatted.

'He'll be quite safe,' I told her. 'The Americans won't drop one of those bombs on British ships, will they?'

'I know,' she said, 'but after Hiroshima and Nagasaki were destroyed, who knows what's next?'

'Papa told me the Japanese will surrender soon,' I said. 'Probably next week.' That last bit was a lie, but I thought it would cheer her up, so it's a little white lie. No harm done, as Alla says.

## August 14th

I must be psychic! I have foretold the future! The Japanese have surrendered! The war's over, throughout the world. Mr Attlee will announce it on the wireless at midnight. Tomorrow will be another day of celebration – VJ Day. That means Victory over Japan.

How wonderful!

And Lilibet had a letter from Philip this morning, so, as Alla said, all's right with her world.

## August 16th

I'm absolutely worn out. We woke yesterday to rain. There was  the State Opening of Parliament before any VJ celebrations. Not even victory throughout the world can stop that! No one cared about the weather, anyway.

Crowds gathered early outside the palace, even more than on VE Day. A report came through that every street in the centre of London was crowded. As the day wore on, there were about a hundred thousand people swarming around outside and along the Mall, Papa reckoned.

Some of the politicians and important army, navy and air force people had dreadful trouble getting into the palace. Even the poor foreign secretary had to use one of the back entrances. He was extremely hot and bothered, Papa said, when he was shown in.

Late in the afternoon the sun shone, and we made several appearances. Lilibet said it almost took her breath away when she stepped on to the balcony and saw the ocean of heads, and felt the warmth of the people and their love for the King.

At nine in the evening, poor Papa had to make a speech. Although it's something he normally loathes, we knew how proud he was to do it on such a day. He asked everyone to remember those who'd died, or who'd lost a loved one, and to remember the suffering of prisoners of war. He ended by saying, '… from the bottom of my heart I thank my peoples for all they have done, not only for themselves but for mankind.' I think he meant that all people, everywhere, are going to have a better future.

Afterwards, when he was having a well-earned drink, Lilibet took my hand and perched on the edge of the sofa, next to him. 'Papa,' she said.

He groaned. 'I know what you're going to ask. Do you have to?'

'It's once in a lifetime,' she said.

'Twice,' he growled. Then he smiled. 'Go on, then, out you go –'

She leapt up. 'And Margaret? Oh, thank you, Papa!'

'Hold on,' he said. 'I want you to come back and tell me who's going with you.'

Soon we were off out in the streets again. This time more people recognized Lilibet than before. It didn't matter, because everyone was so good-natured. I was a little annoyed that hardly anyone noticed me, but I suppose she's in the newspapers more than me.

At one point, remembering how I used to watch her at

Windsor in case a German spy was stalking her, I realized there are probably German spies still in London who've never been caught. Then I looked at the mass of young people, old people, children on shoulders, and thought of the way they cheer us and love us. If any German thought to harm my sister, he'd be spifflicated.

When we finally staggered home it was all I could do to flop in an armchair and drink my hot cocoa.

I kicked my shoes off. 'Oh, Lilibet, wasn't it a wonderful day?'

She sipped her drink. 'It was. In fact,' she said, 'it would have been perfect if Philip had been here to share it, instead of stuck in Tokyo Bay. It can't be much fun there.'

'He'll soon be home,' I said. She looked so lost, so full of longing, I didn't know what else to say.

## August 18th

Lilibet heard that Papa's going to have a meeting with the King of Greece.

'It's to talk about Greece's future now the war's over,' she said. 'Margaret, do you think they'll talk about Philip and me? Oh, they must talk about us.'

169

I took a deep breath. 'Do you really think Papa will be happy about you and Philip – you know, being together? He's got all those German relations, hasn't he?'

'So do we have German relations,' she said, a little snappily, I thought. 'Don't forget that until the First World War our family weren't called Windsor. We belonged to the House of Saxe-Coburg-Gotha. We have plenty of Germans in our family.'

'Yes,' I said patiently, 'but not that sort of German. Not Nazis.'

Lilibet picked up her book and said crossly, 'Anyway, we're not going to be – together – as you put it.'

So there.

## September 3rd

When the news was broadcast that the Japanese had signed the formal surrender document on the American battleship *Missouri*, Lilibet said, 'It's strange to think that Philip's so near that ship, in Tokyo Bay.'

She looked down at her tea cup and I wanted to hug her so badly, but with all the family there, it wouldn't have been a good idea.

## September 16th

Poor Lilibet was thrown from her horse yesterday. She's only bruised, but Mummy never takes chances, and has ordered her to rest. I keep her company as much as I can.

She's been reading piles of magazines. She told me they're beginning to speculate about who she's likely to marry.

'They've suggested a duke, a lord, a Guards officer, Englishmen, an American,' she said. 'And guess who else?'

'Clark Gable? Frank Sinatra? Rumpelstiltskin?'

She laughed.

'Oh, all right then,' I said, 'how about His Royal Highness Prince Philip of Greece?'

Now she blushed!

'It's so silly,' she said. 'I can't imagine why they're interested in something that isn't happening.'

'Don't be daft,' I said. 'You're a pretty princess, who's heir to the British throne – of course they're interested.'

I doubt if they'll be as interested when the time comes for me to marry. I'm just princess number two, and heir to nothing very much. I expect I'll meet someone, fall in love, get married and live happily ever after. That's my plan, anyway.

# October 26th

Lilibet's so busy, we don't meet often, but when we do, we can't stop talking.

After a party the other night, I curled up on the sofa in her sitting room, and we gossiped about everyone. I made her laugh by mimicking one or two (or six!) of the more pompous guests. Sometimes people try to impress us because we're royal, but it never has the right effect. I'm forever grateful that Mummy encouraged us not to let our feelings show. I can generally keep a straight face whatever happens, but not always. My sister's expression never cracks. If some poor soul made an embarrassing noise in front of her, they'd be convinced she hadn't even noticed.

Lilibet said suddenly, 'You know I love Philip, don't you? I know you do.'

I nodded. 'But I haven't said so to anyone, honestly.'

'I didn't think you would,' she said, which pleased me. 'Oh, Margaret, I feel so sorry for girls who don't have a sister.'

So do I.

## November 17th

Lilibet said Mummy picked up the photograph of Philip and said, 'We must have him to stay at Balmoral next summer. What do you think, darling?'

Lilibet told me, 'I was so thrilled that I said, "Oh yes, please," and I think now Mummy knows how I feel.'

I'm quite sure Mummy knew already. And if she does, so does Papa.

## December 23rd

It's lovely to see Papa wind down, as he always does at Sandringham. He looks so thin – 'drawn', Lilibet says.

The one wretched thing that spoils every Christmas is Papa's broadcast. I know he can't relax until it's over, and we're all concerned because he's doing this Christmas message without Mr Logue's help. But he'll get through. He must. We'll all be there with him.

## January 2nd 1946

Lilibet's beside herself with delight, and cannot wait to return to London. Philip's ship, *Whelp*, is being decommissioned, which means she'll no longer be on active service. This takes time, so she'll be in Portsmouth for a couple of months, and who's in charge of the decommissioning? Philip!

'I should see him often,' Lilibet told me. 'Portsmouth isn't a million miles away from London, and he's sure to be staying in Uncle Dickie's house in Chester Street.'

## January 3rd

Our poor, darling Alla has died. She's been ill, but we didn't realize how serious it was. I can't imagine our lives without her. Mummy's terribly upset. Alla was her nanny, too, when she was young.

I'm so glad we still have Bobo and Ruby. And Crawfie, of course. Oh dear, I keep crying. It's such a shock.

Papa still looks so worn. He was more cheerful now he's had a relaxing little holiday, but he's upset about Alla, too.

## January 24th

Even though war's over, food is still rationed. When we drive through London, there are always queues everywhere.

Lilibet often tells me how lucky we are to be driven everywhere, or to travel in the royal train. 'We don't have to sit in rows pressed up against other people,' she says. 'We don't have to queue for our bread.'

I wish she wouldn't say things like that. I know how fortunate I am. I don't need to be told. When I was little I used to envy girls who could play with their friends in gardens or streets. And I know many girls would love to be a princess like me. But they don't realize it can be lonely living in a palace, even though there are people at every door and in every corridor. They're not people you can play with, or sit and gossip with, or dance to the gramophone with. I suppose we all want what we can't have.

Philip's in Portsmouth, and every weekend he zooms up to Chester Street in his little MG sports car, so he often comes to lunch, and to parties. Lilibet's in seventh heaven when that happens and spends hours getting ready!

The only drawback is that Philip's photograph is sometimes in the newspapers because he goes to fashionable nightclubs in the West End, and often there are beautiful girls in the background. That's not nice for my sister. He has a cousin called David, and I think they have a good time together. Lilibet would so love to be with Philip, but you can't have a royal princess whirling round the dance floor in a nightclub!

## March 1st

Oh golly gosh! I've known it was coming, but I keep putting it out of my mind. I've an official engagement of my very own on the 26th. On my own! I'll have people with me, of course, but I'm doing the opening alone. It's a play centre in Camden, called the Hopscotch Inn. I don't have to make a speech, just declare it open, and chat to people. I hope I do it well.

## March 26th

Lilibet said she's very proud of me, because everyone says what a fine job I did opening the play centre. I kept smiling, and shook every hand I saw, and watched the children playing and asked questions – sensible ones, I hope!

## April 19th

Poor Lilibet hoped Philip would come to her birthday celebration, but he's visiting friends in Paris. Shame. Papa knows she's missing him. He doesn't say anything, but he pats her shoulder as he passes. What does he think? Does he imagine Philip might propose to Elizabeth one day? Does he mind?

## May 25th

Yesterday was Empire Day. Lilibet made a speech and in it she hinted at something exciting. Next spring, we – the four of us – are going to South Africa! For Lilibet and me it will be our first visit abroad. We'll be away three or four months. I'm so excited.

## June 3rd

Philip's now a teacher! He trains petty officers at HMS *Royal Arthur* in Wiltshire. It's amazing to think that when we first met him, he was being trained, and now he's training others.

He's going to join us at Balmoral this summer, so Lilibet's walking on air.

# July 26th

Lilibet has been to stay at Coppins, Aunt Marina's home. And who should happen to be there at the same time? None other than Prince Philip!

She comes back from those visits with her head in the clouds. Nine times out of ten, when I go to her sitting room, she's playing, 'People Will Say We're in Love' on her gramophone.

'Margaret,' she said one day, gripping both my hands so tightly they hurt. 'I'm going to marry Philip!'

'Has Papa given permission?'

'No,' she said, 'and you mustn't say anything. Promise me you won't?'

I crossed my heart. 'Of course not.'

'You see, Philip hasn't proposed. Not yet. Oh, I'm sure he will,' she said, and went to gaze out of the window.

I do hope he does. He'll make a very good brother-in-law. And as I've never had a brother, he'll do nicely.

But I've a horrid feeling Papa won't be happy. Imagine. The future queen, engaged to a man with no home, no money, no close family, and those sisters, married to Germans.

Oh dear.

# August 9th

Here we are at Balmoral. Sunny days, fresh air, and all together.

What's even better is that Lilibet has a permanent smile! Anyone could see she's in love. But does Philip love her? Really love her? He's very attentive, and the other day I saw them holding hands, but that's all. I've never seen them kiss or anything.

Philip told me he's not mad about Balmoral. 'All that ruddy tartan,' he said, 'chilly rooms, animals' heads on the walls. Whole place needs modernizing.'

That was a bit rich, considering he doesn't even have a home. He also doesn't have proper clothes – not ones suitable for Balmoral. He wears old shoes, and when Lilibet pulled the back of his dinner jacket straight, he said, 'No use fussing – it doesn't fit. It's Uncle Dickie's.' His pockets are permanently saggy, because he always stuffs his hands in them – except when he's holding my sister's hand, tee hee!

## August 10th

Philip nearly had me in stitches tonight. He wore a kilt for the first time, and when he was shown into the drawing room where Papa was waiting, he pretended to curtsey. The King was not amused, but I was!

Actually, although Papa obviously likes him, I think Philip gets on his nerves sometimes. He doesn't think before he speaks, and he behaves as I imagine he would with his fellow officers. It doesn't go down well in our dining room, that's for sure. I can see Lilibet getting anxious sometimes, as if she dreads what he'll come out with next! I think he ought to consider her feelings.

Philip's also rubbed one of Papa's equerries up the wrong way. I don't think he and Philip like each other much. I hope he doesn't say anything bad to Papa. I've a sneaking suspicion that Papa's secretary isn't keen, either.

# August 12th

Ooh, I'm bubbling with excitement! Lilibet practically fell into my room last night.

'What d'you think, Margaret? What d'you think?'

I patted my bed. 'Tell me!' I sort of guessed, but in case I hadn't guessed right, I didn't want to say the wrong thing.

She clasped her hands together. 'Philip proposed!'

I threw my arms round her. 'Oh, Lilibet, I'm so happy for you. What did he say? Tell me everything!'

I know what authors mean when they say someone's eyes were shining. 'He loves me,' she said. 'He wants to spend the rest of his life with me, and there'll never be anyone else for him. Oh, Margaret, I'm the happiest girl in the world!'

I looked innocent. 'Did you give him an answer?'

She grabbed a pillow and hit me over the head with it. Then her smile faded. 'Do you think Papa will give his permission?'

I stared at her. 'You mean you've said yes, and Papa doesn't even know?' I believe that's normal for ordinary girls, but Lilibet is a royal princess and heir to the throne. She could never marry – nor could I – without the King's permission.

She nibbled her lip. 'They do like Philip, I know they do.'

'They like the footmen who walk the dogs, but they'd never consider you marrying one of them!'

We both laughed.

'Everything will be fine. You'll see,' I said. 'Make Philip talk to Papa tomorrow.'

## August 19th

Lilibet is quite tense, except when she's with Philip. He's spoken to Papa, and there have been a lot of talks. As far as I can gather, Philip intends (if he marries Lilibet) to give up his Greek titles.

'Who needs a title in the navy?' he said to Lilibet. 'It sets you apart from your men. Not a good thing.'

## August 26th

Still no permission from Papa.

I think, but I'm not sure, that the plan is for Philip to

take the Mountbatten surname. His grandfather was Prince Louis of Battenberg, and the Battenbergs were German. Prince Louis gave up his titles in 1917, changed his name to Mountbatten, and was created the Marquess of Milford Haven by my grandfather, George V.

This new name will make Philip appear less foreign to the British people. It's a jolly good thing he hasn't taken the name of the royal house he belongs to: Schleswig-Holstein-Sonderburg-Glücksburg!

Philip seems cheerful and relaxed, so things must be going the right way. But then he always is cheerful and relaxed. He has a jokey remark for every occasion. Sometimes, his comments seem almost rude, but they're always funny. They're the sort that make you splutter.

## August 28th

Papa insists the engagement must be kept secret for now. Lilibet agreed, of course, but I know she's bursting for the world to know that they're in love.

Mummy says the most important consideration is that Philip is kind to Lilibet, and faithful, and that he learns to become a good consort. When Lilibet is queen, he must support her in every way – that's a consort's role.

If Philip remained a prince, he'd become the prince consort. 'You can't very well have a lieutenant consort, can you, Mummy?' I said. 'Won't it be rather odd?'

She laughed. 'Quite right, darling. But Papa will sort that out.'

## September 4th

Greece are to have the monarchy back after all these years, and Philip's cousin, George II, is to be restored to the Greek throne. He knows about the romance, and Papa is worried he'll let out the news of the engagement.

## September 7th

The news is out. That didn't take long. There was a report in the paper today, saying that Princess Elizabeth is to become engaged to a distant cousin, Prince Philip of Greece and Denmark.

'How infuriating!' Mummy said. I know she believes it was King George who let the news slip. 'Well, we'll see about that.'

Papa immediately told his private secretary to issue a denial of 'the rumours'.

Lilibet's miserable. The shine's being taken off her happiness.

'It's only words,' I said. 'You know what newspapers are like.'

I know why she's unhappy. It's all a lie, and she's an honest, straightforward person. But sometimes lies are necessary. A royal engagement and marriage must be done properly and, anyway, Papa feels this isn't the right time.

## September 11th

The result of the newspaper leak is a poll showing that not all the British people would be happy to see the elder daughter of their king marrying someone with strong German connections. It's too soon after the war.

## October 27th

Lilibet and I were bridesmaids at Pamela Mountbatten's wedding at Romsey Abbey yesterday, and Philip was an usher.

We had to hold flowers and keep our skirts out of puddles and when we went to take off our fur coats, Philip fairly leapt to help Lilibet. Then he helped me (good old number two princess!).

The thing was, there was quite a buzz from the spectators when that happened. Newspaper photographers clicked their cameras madly, and I heard the whirr of a film camera.

Afterwards, Lilibet said, 'I wish we could announce the engagement and get it over with.'

'Well, you can't,' I said. 'Philip's going to become a British citizen first. Those things don't happen overnight. Anyway, your engagement ring won't be ready for ages.'

Philip's having the ring made using diamonds from his mother's tiara. I expect that's because he can't afford one himself, but I think it's romantic that Lilibet will wear something all her life that belonged to Philip's mother. Also, when she gets married, it'll fulfil part of the 'something old, something new, something borrowed, something blue' tradition.

## November 1st

We had such a grand evening. We went in a big party to a Royal Film Performance. It was held to raise money for a charity that benefits needy people, like widows or the sick, from the film and television world. It's nice that such a fun evening helps people. We all hope it becomes a regular event!

The film we saw was *A Matter of Life and Death*. Lots of stars were there, and they shone searchlights into the sky. Leicester Square was packed with people. All we royal ladies were given bouquets by sweet little children. How they stared at us! As we entered our box, there was a fanfare of trumpets, which made me jump. It was a lovely evening, and the only thing wrong was that we were slow getting through the traffic and crowds and Papa got a little bad-tempered. I think he still gets tired. I wish his cough was better. But the hold-up didn't spoil the evening, which was wonderful except for the usual complaint. Philip isn't here.

## November 5th

Another fantastic evening. Oh, I do love London. Now the war's over, it seems that there's always something wonderful to look forward to. Tonight it was the Royal Command Variety Performance at the Palladium Theatre. It was so thrilling. Our box was decorated with loads of flowers.

'No gardenias,' whispered Mummy. 'At least Margaret won't sneeze all the way through.'

'No,' Lilibet whispered back. 'She'll just fidget.'

Cheek!

A drumroll signalled the national anthem, then a spotlight shone on Mummy and Papa. Every head in the audience craned to see us! Why do I always feel a giggle coming on at times like that? Nerves, Lilibet says.

## December 2nd

I bet we have a white Christmas. I've never known the weather so cold.

Philip will come to Sandringham. That'll be fun, because he's great at joining in. He's tall, too, so he can help decorate the tree, so I don't have to climb the ladder, which I don't care for.

His Christmas invitation is another sign that everything's proceeding well, though nothing can be taken for granted where royal life is concerned.

In a few weeks we four will leave for our South African visit. My first trip abroad. I'm so excited. It'll be lovely and warm, I know. Ruby and Bobo are in a flurry of lists and dress fittings and jewellery checks. Lilibet's so looking forward to Christmas but, although she longs to see South Africa, she'd rather not leave Philip behind. If only the engagement could be made official before we go, but it can't. I just hope they get on with making Philip a British citizen. Papa's given his permission for that, and Philip's delighted because, as a citizen, he can have a proper career in our navy.

## December 11th

Mummy and I had lunch by ourselves today. It's so cold we had to send for warm cardigans. She asked if I'm excited about the trip.

'Very,' I said. 'I just wish Lilibet wasn't sad about leaving Philip.'

'It'll be fine when we're there,' said Mummy. 'So many new things to see – it will be a distraction for her. She'll barely have time to think of Philip.' She sipped a glass of water. 'In fact, it will give them both a chance to decide if they're doing the right thing.'

I put down my knife and fork and folded my arms.

'Darling, we don't mean to be difficult about the engagement,' said Mummy. 'There are some members of the household and the government who believe that the people won't accept Philip. In fact, there's been another horrid poll in the newspaper. About fifty-five per cent of the people think it's a good idea, but forty per cent are against it.'

'You mean because of the German thing?'

Mummy nodded.

'But the war's over,' I said. 'Shouldn't we forgive and forget? After all, Philip was on our side. He didn't go round shooting down Spitfires, did he?'

She laughed.

## January 14th 1947

The whole palace is in a going-away fluster. Lilibet's sulking because Papa told Philip he can't come on board our ship to say goodbye.

'We'll be gone for ten weeks,' she said angrily. 'It's such a little thing to ask.'

'It's the little thing that would give the game away to newspaper reporters,' I said.

She couldn't argue with that and, to be fair, she's been careful not to be seen in public with Philip.

'Anyway,' I went on, 'he's having a lovely farewell dinner party for us in Chester Street. Did you know he's inviting

Noël Coward? I'm busy learning all his songs in case I get a chance to sing with him.'

'Margaret, you wouldn't!' she said.

I would.

## January 16th

Lilibet and I have studied the map and looked at all the exotic names of places we might be visiting: Bloemfontein, Basutoland, Swaziland, Bechuanaland, Natal.

'Here's a good name,' said Lilibet, pointing. 'Port Elizabeth.'

'Port Margaret would sound nicer,' I said.

'Ha ha!'

I immediately broke into the song I've been driving Lilibet mad with, 'Carry me back to the old Transvaal, That's where I long to be…'

She covered her ears. 'All right, Port Margaret would be wonderful! Anyway, we can hardly carry you back to the old Transvaal when you haven't even been there!'

We're travelling by air, rail and road. Won't it be lovely to be in sunshine after this terrible cold winter. Mummy says she's never known it to be so bitter, and she's Scottish.

Papa feels bad leaving Britain, because there are so many problems caused by the weather, but Mummy says he's looking forward to the trip. He probably realizes that if Lilibet marries, it could be the last time we four are together.

## January 21st

Huge snowfalls everywhere. Roads blocked. It looks so beautiful out of our windows, but people are suffering. I hope we can get to Portsmouth to board our ship.

## February 2nd

We're on our way! We left Buckingham Palace in the snow and drove out with the Household Cavalry trotting alongside, looking so smart. Crowds waved us all the way to Waterloo, where we boarded the train for Portsmouth.

On the way, we peered into people's gardens, and in many there were grown-ups and children waving Union Jacks.

They'd waited outside in the cold for us to whizz past. We couldn't believe how kind people are.

Portsmouth was even colder than London, with a biting, sleety wind. When I tried to speak, my lips wouldn't work properly. But once we'd boarded the *Vanguard*, endured a forty-one-gun salute and waved to some of the naval and private ships who'd gathered to see us off, we were cosy enough.

## On HMS Vanguard

Ooooh, I never want to see the Bay of Biscay ever again. Not that I saw much this time, because I could barely move from my bed. Seasickness is the nastiest thing. Poor Lilibet was worse than me; she said she wanted to die. Mummy couldn't move, and Papa stayed with her.

But when the rough seas settled, how different everything became! Papa's now wearing tropical clothes. Lilibet and I are in cotton dresses, but Mummy still dresses in her own glamorous way.

You can do rifle shooting on this ship. We've all had a go and I'm pretty good at it, better than Lilibet!

We all play games, and the officers join in. Philip would be livid if he saw how much they all like Lilibet and what fun she's having with them! Such a flirt!

Papa's had reports about how bad the British weather is. I think he feels guilty that he's in sunshine while everyone at home is freezing. He said there are twenty-foot snowdrifts in some places, and whole villages are cut off. There's a lot of flu about, too, and people are dying. Papa's such a caring king.

Lilibet told me Philip will become a British citizen on February 28th, but it won't be announced straight away. I think then she'll put pressure on Papa to agree to a formal engagement. He doesn't like being pushed, so she must be careful. I do think he looks a little better now – not so thin and exhausted. The rest and sunshine are doing him good. Mummy just basks under a parasol and laughs at all of us.

## Our visit to South Africa

The weather was glorious when we first sighted Cape Town. Table Mountain is a strange sight, with its long flat top. It had a layer of cloud over it, looking for all the world like a tablecloth.

The heat got to us after a couple of days. We're just not used to it. Mummy uses a parasol or umbrella when we're riding in open cars in blazing sunshine. She'd hate her face to get sunburnt.

We've hardly had a moment to ourselves! The weeks are flying by. There have been audiences with important people, garden parties, balls, opening parliament, pageants... We walked for about a mile through dripping, steamy forest to visit the Victoria Falls, we've seen strange animals and brilliantly-coloured birds, and it's so hot. Whenever we get where we're going, all we want to do is flop, but first there's the national anthem, which we have to stand for, of course, and they always sing every verse.

Some of the highlights: when there was a storm in a town we visited, and the people thought we were bringers-of-rain! Being allowed to ride with the train driver and pulling the whistle! Visiting an ostrich farm, seeing baby ostriches (ugly) and being given an egg (huge). Hearing the official news of Philip becoming British and, first, seeing Lilibet's delighted smile and then recognizing a determined look in her eye that said, 'Now then, Papa…' And horse riding on wide, empty beaches! All so exciting and new!

Not everything was good. King George of Greece died while we were away, and his brother Paul assumed the throne. Papa has been quite short-tempered. He roared at our driver one day, and he was furious with me when I laughed at a lady's curtsey – I felt bad when he pointed out to me that she was clumsy because her joints were stiff and painful. Then I laughed at an African chief when he tripped over his words. That was really, really bad. Lilibet said I should have known better, being the daughter of someone who has problems with public speaking. When I remember that day I feel ashamed.

Mummy has a memory that makes her feel uncomfortable. A Zulu man ran at our car, shouting and waving his arm. Papa yelled at the driver to speed up, and Mummy bravely hit the man over the head with her parasol. The police dragged him away. The awful thing was that later we learned he was only trying to give Lilibet a ten-shilling note as an early birthday present. We all felt sick when we heard. Lilibet was terribly upset. 'I must write to him,' she said, but unfortunately we don't know where he is. It's such a sad, but sweet story.

On Lilibet's twenty-first birthday, she sat in front of a microphone at a small table in the shade and broadcast a message to the Commonwealth. In it, she dedicated her whole life, whether it be long or short, to our people and to the service of the Empire. She looked so lovely, and sounded so sincere, and when she said 'whether it be long or short', I had to swallow hard. Her life is going to be what Mummy calls 'a challenge'.

She had some breathtaking presents: lots of diamonds – after all, this is a diamond-mining country – her final two pearls, a gold key to Cape Town, and presents from all the family and the royal household. What brought the biggest smile to her face was a telegram from Philip, which she refused to show to anybody. They spoke on the telephone, too, and when she'd finished, I hugged her and we didn't speak.

# Going home

Eventually, there was a farewell luncheon, when we all received jewels, and Mummy was given a gold tea service. They were terribly generous.

We waved goodbye to beautiful South Africa, and then it was back on the *Vanguard*, very tired, and glad of some peace and quiet. Poor Papa seems as tired as he was when we left England, and looks much thinner to me. He needs rest.

I think Lilibet would gladly have taken an oar and rowed if it would have helped us get back any faster! But even when we reached Portsmouth, there were greetings and cannon salutes and inspections and flowers and a civic reception. Then a peaceful train ride to Waterloo where we were greeted by the prime minister and other dignitaries, then into a carriage. Oh, it was so good to cross the Thames and see the dear old Palace of Westminster again. There must have been thousands on the streets, welcoming us home. Westminster Bridge itself was lined with well-wishers. Then, back to the palace for a balcony appearance, and all the time, Lilibet must have been bursting to rush home and telephone Philip.

# May 14th

Everything's back to normal for me, but my sister's in a whirl!
She's always out at parties or the theatre, or even nightclubs,
where I'm not allowed to go. Just wait till I'm eighteen! I'll
have such a good time.

Lilibet sometimes comes to see me in the morning to tell
me all about the night before. I must say, she always seems
to have young men crowding round her. Philip had better
watch out! I'm sure Mummy and Papa are encouraging her
to mix with all these young men (from good families, of
course). She enjoys flirting. But I know her heart belongs
to Philip.

I joined Papa for a stroll in the warm night air after dinner
last night. Lilibet was out for the evening, and Mummy had a
headache. The dogs all followed us out, of course.

I took a deep breath. 'Papa, are you going to announce
Lilibet's engagement to Philip?'

He was quiet for a moment. 'If I announce it, it will be
official, and there'll be no going back.'

He sat down heavily on a bench overlooking the lake. I
sat beside him, picked up his arm and hooked it round my

shoulders, like I used to do when I was little. He patted my hand. 'Margaret, I still don't know if he's right for her.'

'Why not?' I asked.

'I don't know. He's a terrific chap and all that, but he'd be marrying into a life that he's just not used to. Not fitted for. He's used to going where he pleases, when he pleases, sailing, cricket, nightclubs, all that sort of thing.'

'But if he marries, he'll change, won't he?'

Papa gazed up through the branches of a horse chestnut tree. 'Will he? I don't know.'

'Then why not ask him?'

Papa smiled and kissed the tip of my nose. 'What a good idea!'

I don't know if he meant that, or if he was really laughing at me.

## May 15th

Papa has to make a speech at the Guildhall today. His cough is bad, and his voice isn't strong. I hope it doesn't wear him out.

# May 24th

Lilibet wants to talk to Papa about the engagement, but she keeps putting it off, because he's clearly exhausted. Only one thing keeps the smile on her face. The day after tomorrow Queen Mary's having a luncheon party here at the palace, to celebrate her eightieth birthday. Philip's been invited.

'That has to be a good sign, doesn't it, Margaret?' she whispered, as we waited to meet some charity officials for a reception. 'If Granny approves of Philip, I mean?'

'Ssh,' I hissed. I didn't want us to get black looks for talking at the wrong time. But then I leaned towards her and whispered, 'If Papa had decided against him, he definitely wouldn't be coming, would he, so it is a good sign.'

That earned me a look from Mummy. How she can show she's cross at the same time as giving a beaming smile beats me, but she can.

# June 13th

Lots of engagements – Trooping the Colour yesterday, for the first time since 1939, and the crowds were out in force.

Lilibet has been given the freedom of the City of London. I went to the ceremony with her on Wednesday. She inspected a guard of honour first, then received the most gigantic bouquet. You could hardly see her behind them. 'No gardenias,' she whispered to me. After photographs, we went inside. The prime minister was there. The declaration announced that she's the first royal princess to accept the honour. It was formal, but friendly at the same time.

We have both (me, too!) been appointed by Papa to the Imperial Order of the Crown of India. I imagine we're the very last members, as India is shortly becoming independent. The insignia has the letters VRI (Victoria Regina Imperatrix) set with jewels, and it's on a pretty light-blue bow. Maybe one day I might go to India, and wear it there.

Lilibet has so many engagements now. She's happy to do them, because they relieve Papa of a lot of duties. She's always glad when I go along, too.

Papa usually has Mummy to accompany him. How could

Lilibet face the prospect of being queen without having somebody of her own to help and support her. She needs her Philip. She loves him.

## July 1st

The moment came when Papa was ready to talk about Philip. He sent everyone away except Lilibet and Mummy. I practically wore a groove in the carpet, because I paced up and down so much. I trod on two paws and was so anxious that I wouldn't have noticed if the poor dogs hadn't yelped.

Finally everyone came out, and I dived for the sofa so it wouldn't look as if I was lurking. They smiled at each other as they talked about it being time for coffee, but there was something in the air.

As soon as I could get her alone, I said to Lilibet, 'Well?'

'I just don't know,' she said miserably. 'Papa said he's thought of nothing else, and seemed to have come round to the idea, but Mummy's clearly still not sure. She said she's fond of Philip, but…'

'But what?'

'That's just it. She didn't seem able to express how she feels. Oh, Margaret, I can't bear it.'

# July 2nd

I managed to get Mummy and Papa alone this morning.

'You love Mummy, don't you, Papa?' I said.

'Of course I do.'

'You had to ask her to marry you more than once before she accepted, didn't you?'

'Yes, but I'd rather you didn't tell anyone that.'

'I won't, but why wouldn't you take no for an answer?'

He smiled at Mummy. 'I knew she was right for me.'

'Well, then,' I said. 'Lilibet knows Philip's right for her. Don't you see?'

They looked at each other.

'She'll be queen one day,' I said. 'She needs Philip. I know him. I know he'll never let her down. He'll be the best consort ever. You have to let her marry him.'

Slowly, Mummy raised a finger to her lips. I knew what she meant. Nobody, not even a princess, tells a king what he must or mustn't do. But I dared.

Papa came over to where I sat. He crouched in front of me, and said, 'Margaret, Lilibet is a very lucky young woman. She'll never want for love and support while she has you.'

My eyes became teary, but I held it back.

'Trust me,' he said. 'I'll do whatever's best for Lilibet's happiness.'

And he did.

## July 9th

Today, I watched proudly as the King and Queen announced the engagement of their dearly beloved daughter, the Princess Elizabeth to Lieutenant Philip Mountbatten, RN.

And they'll live happily ever after – my sister Lilibet and her prince, Philip.

## THE END

Experience history first-hand with My Story –
a series of vividly imagined accounts of life in the past.

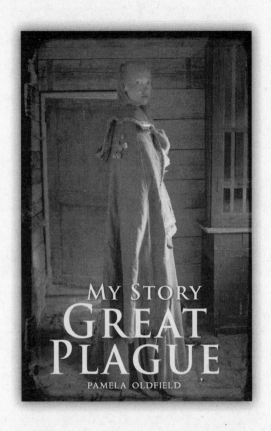

MY STORY
GREAT
PLAGUE
PAMELA OLDFIELD

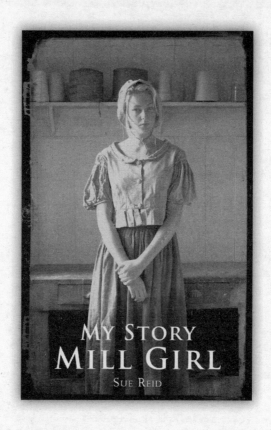

## MY STORY
# MILL GIRL

Sue Reid

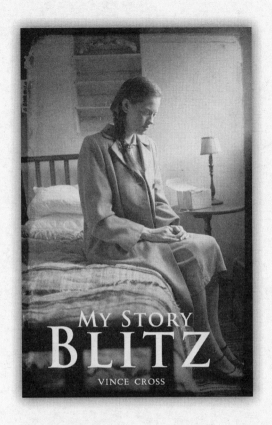

My Story

# BLITZ

VINCE CROSS

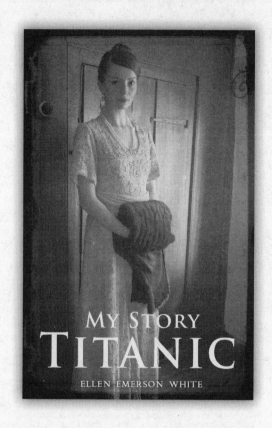

# MY STORY
# TITANIC

ELLEN EMERSON WHITE

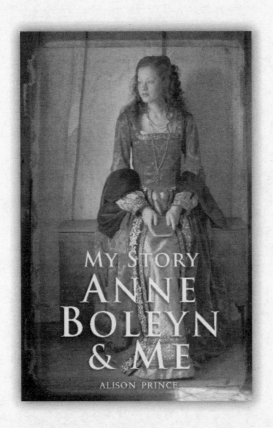

My Story

ANNE
BOLEYN
& ME

ALISON PRINCE

# MY STORY
# POMPEII

Sue Reid

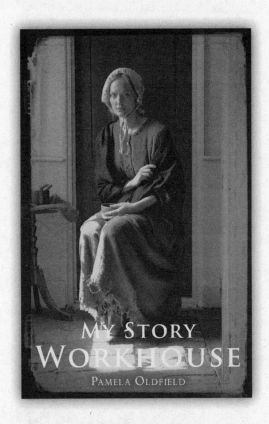

## My Story
# WORKHOUSE
### Pamela Oldfield

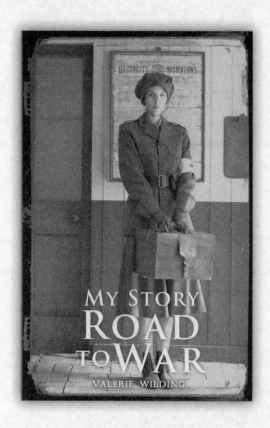

# My Story
# ROAD
# to WAR

VALERIE WILDING

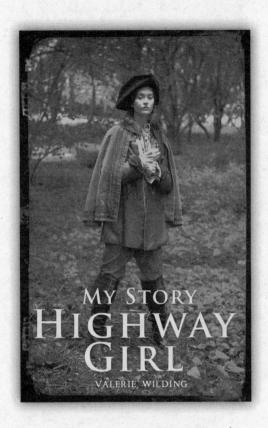

## My Story
# HIGHWAY
# GIRL
### VALERIE WILDING

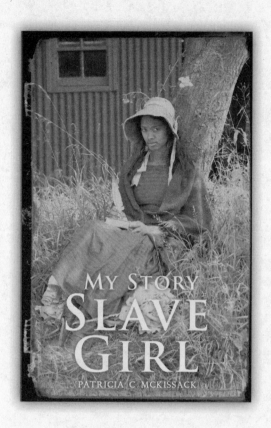

My Story

SLAVE
GIRL

PATRICIA C MCKISSACK

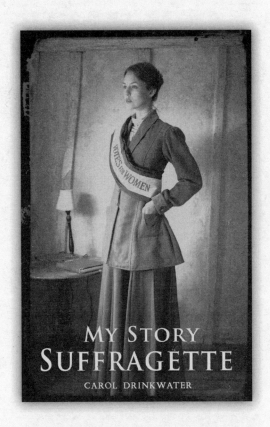

# MY STORY
# SUFFRAGETTE

CAROL DRINKWATER

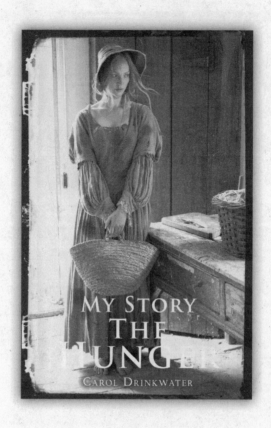

MY STORY
THE HUNGER
CAROL DRINKWATER